WING ME OVER THE SEA

Wing Me Over The Sea

A novel
by

JUDYTH EMANUEL

BOOKS
Adelaide Books
New York/Lisbon
2020

WING ME OVER THE SEA
A novel
By Judyth Emanuel

Published by Adelaide Books, New York / Lisbon
adelaidebooks.org

Editor-in-Chief
Stevan V. Nikolic

For any information, please address Adelaide Books
at info@adelaidebooks.org
or write to:
Adelaide Books
244 Fifth Ave. Suite D27
New York, NY, 10001

ISBN-10: 1-949180-16-6
ISBN-13: 978-1-949180-16-9

Printed in the United States of America

Contents

TRAVEL

NOTES

AND

STORIES

OF

INNOVATIVE

REALITY

This day is nice *when I wake.* Yawn.

A blimp of fear bursts out from me. *Help.*

Things change color.

The whole world unbuttons.

The people of the earth are lovely.

The places of the earth are lovely.

And I am not frightened anymore.

1

go   the   world

Notes

It is an inexpressible pleasure to know a little of the world and be of no significance in it. **Montaigne, chapters eleven, eighteen, twenty-five.**

When strangers look at each other what do they glimpse?

Tell the world where you've been.....oh I've traveled and observed curiosities. Random scenes that capture the character of a country. The trivial memories of traveling and retelling, rereading looking closely at holiday snaps posted on the internet for anyone to steal, gives me an astonishing sense of being myself, reliving that life again,
scribble

    silly

        baffle

Don't be stuffy.

Get the hell outta here wherever you are. Go. Plane Train Car Walk Run Swim. Simple. To be or not. And find yourself in another place. Being not being for the ambiguity.

Maybe fly to the moon. Drive a shiny rocket. Can I? In dark glasses. Wearing velvet slippers. Guess what? Imagine the cheese. Space brie and moonrock cheddar. How high must I launch myself? Scary for Bliss, (I am Bliss) a vertically challenged big terror of flight woman. Going up, says the recorded message, *gawd* vertigo is there such a thing? Wait and see. Can you just see me?

The desire to travel grips anyone, not only Bliss but also my friend Winky, who I also sleep with. No definition for that kind of trip, maybe the final one. When we are dead.

Bliss. A short woman, hip and plump, pushing fifty. Okay disorganized, brushes marriage aside, brushing brown hair, a windswept mop framing a round face, fluttering grey eyes of contented lines fan out, far out freckles and him. Winky. Round of bald slippery and a belly like Buddha. There we be body mix. A burble melts into podge like a cul-de-sac and a splotch of motor oil. We Are The Road. I Am The Journey. But.

Bliss and Winky unadventurous in an adventurous way, sometimes tentative explorers, must be brave, be braver. Experience extraordinary places. I think, but not too strange. Not heroic. An easy daring. A fraction gutsy. Bravery and guts. And when we return home from a trip, I begin dreaming of going somewhere else. The destination unimportant. Okay, a tiny bit important. Cool climates, clean sheets, a view, maybe doughnuts. And decent coffee.

Where does a journey begin and end? Is it. On the way. At the destination. Back home. Who cares? Anywhere new

Inflames The Senses.

Here *here.* The meaning of traveling what it is and why we do it. Why tell me *why.* See below.

My wings. The wind beneath. That kind of fluff.

My teacher tells me never to use the word 'beneath.' But it's such a beautiful word. The wind beneath. My Wings. She arrives ten minutes late and leaves ten minutes early for classes costing one hundred and fifty dollars for three hours. I wear fabulous shoes and my teacher dresses like Pippi Longstocking. She doesn't like me.

But I am wandering away from.

What Is Vital? Any place but here! The boredom of sameness, the limitations of 'home' create a requirement to 'get away' and land without a bump in a foreign country, another language, do you understand what I am saying, it's boring at home, living here most of my life. Don't get me started or I will take you back to the moment I first open my eyes in a squinty way only to decide everything here is dull.

The obvious reason why we travel to *other* lands. Cities mostly or the countryside, rows of grapevines, dams, waterfalls the size of skyscrapers, bogs I'm not sure where, swamps in sticky places, and always the unfamiliar igniting Love and Friendship and Bliss.

Therefore. Go   The   World. Expensive or cheap, what you can afford, the new, the different, the mind-blowing, no matter how mundane proves freaking extraordinary. Again, obvious and no one needs convincing. Right, you say, but everyone goes on a journey and you are not that unusual.

I close my eyes. I can't tell where we are by closing my eyes. I open my eyes. Oh the places of the earth are lovely. Yes. The people of the earth are lovely.

But what's in store for me in the direction I don't take?

Definitions Of Tripping

Trips define the tripping. Like walking to the corner store. Buy a loaf of bread, a packet of Custard Creams, a couple of gobstoppers, the essentials, any trip becomes essential, where are we going, you won't know until you go. That kind of a trip. This trip. Winky takes Bliss to the movies. He buys her a choc-top. Full stop.

And this particular classification of tripping comes from an unlikely source you understand and the words have a certain quaint momentum. So obscure, these romantic quotes, I nicked from a strain of Old English Folk-Speak.

Lawk a massey! Dwon 'ee tell I that, ur I shall drow't aal up agean! An' none on us dursen zaay no more to un, a look'd so guly, we was aveard as he 'ood.

Write these words down.
Truckle, tuffin, flirk, cribble,
bittle, shitabed,

trumping. Hakketty,
storm-cock, liver-sand,
spick, pig-haw.

Don't you love all of the above? Whoa gives me cribble.

Listen. Let me tell you in brief, here, right now, more Folk-Speak tripping means, the 'take-off' in jumping. Simple idea. A tripper leaps into the unknown. A tripper trips here and there, different spots, la la la.

And these our journeys of us being Winky and Bliss (me) sometimes blind. Well because my tripping speed dial runs too quick. Sometimes the landing is just fucking terrible. Sometimes, I find myself in a better place than the actual tripping. And lose myself in the Innovative Reality of a trip. Usually backwards.

But I remember less than nothing. Rolling stone Bliss, her affliction of memory loss. Moss-covered memories. Vague memories accumulate and I jot down post conceptual notes. Archivist quirks connecting inconsequential wonders. Is this interesting? Random? Shocking? Not really. Do you care? If the answer is no, don't tell me.

I wonder at going beyond, into the preserve of what happens. Which makes me the bumble, the doddle, the dodging, the whining spectator, the self as a wandering robot switching off the desk lamp and heaving myself out of the chair and heading for the next beyond.

My notes will be a reincarnation of the past. The open sesame flipping show us the light. Not really the pilgrimage, but a shuffle into hyperbole. Illusion versus dullness. A contaminated freak exhibition, this awakening to whatever happens. Ha. The blind lady asks, are you laughing? Yes. Can you see? Of course. Only the sightless see.

I recall figures marching in circles inside clocks on the facades of ornate buildings and gazing up at five hundred miles from reality. For what is real. Yes this pizza.

And then comes the voluptuousness of accumulation. What we bring home. Anything to declare? The forged letter I show immigration officers. This crap? These are all genuine souvenirs.

A hoarder, scrupulous in preserving mementos, hoards bits and bobs. A rolling stone gathers cards, and whatnot, tickets and brochures, postcards, fridge magnets, receipts, random paper tokens and maps all of which Bliss keeps forever. Ho ho ho.

I sort through piles of clutter signifying countries visited, stayed in, lived in and dreamed of in wonder. *Bliss*. Imagine such places!

Right now I think Kerouac is cringing. Not everyone specifically wants to jump freight trains. Some people prefer hire cars.

And I have an Imagination. The alternative to crude slaphappy reality you know, the tangible experience.

I have Proof of A Life beyond all imaginings. Look hundreds of fridge magnets! Show and Tell. Kitsch keepsakes, four to six dollars, pounds, francs, pesos. Currency spent on toys to maintain a memory.

Let me show you. Some of my magnets. The Everglades crocodile, the mosaic elephant from the Natural History Museum, a miniature crate containing six bottles of wine from France, a set of replica front covers from The New Yorker, Argentinian tango dancers, brightly colored houses from Valparaiso, the Stuart Clan Scottish tartan and The Empire State building.

Okay, tourist trash. Fridge magnets refusing to stick to my fake stainless steel refrigerator door. Failed magnets.

Inhospitable refrigerator. Except the magnet from NASA, stuck to the metal base of a lamp on my desk. What astronauts believe.

Failure Is Not An Option.

More rubbish I keep. A royal blue leaflet. On the front page, two lines of gold type under the symbol of a golden crown.

Welcome To Palace of Holyroodhouse
Visitor Information.

Err, sorry, no recollection of Holyroodhouse. I squint my special squint at the few illustrations. The quadrangle? The Abbey ruins? The forecourt? The Queen's Gallery? Nope. My mind fizzles like a damp candle wick. Not a flicker. On the back page of the brochure in black type, a command,

Keep In Touch.

I can do that.

Dig out a map of The Lion Forest Garden in Suzhou. There are no lions in the pavilions, halls and towers. The Sleeping-Cloud Room, The Standing-In-Snow Hall, The True-Delight Pavilion. Do we notice any clouds asleep? Do we stand in the snow and feel true delight? Probably. Almost. Yes. Try to remember. *Try.*

I sit at a window, my elbows on the sill and stare through glass. In the distance an old fort, fishing boats in a port, waves crashing the usual crash on rocks, the setting sun shall I go to a bar, vodka on the rocks. Always the same question. Where am I?

Sometimes a solitary journey, I am Bliss ever the outsider, lacking bravado, hungry, shy standing outside cafes filled with chatter, convivial brunchers deep in good conversations, pastries, espressos, happiness. Just out of reach.

Go inside for fucks sake. But in my personality trapping me, I remain unreachable. That is until I begin to travel with Winky.

The world's so dark without you…

Winky the intrepid traveler, he perseveres, thirsting for a challenge, setting out to the remotest, far-flung, highest place. Climbs the steep stairs to the top of the loftiest pagoda. Drives from Key Largo to Key West. So many Keys. Rodriguez Key, Cotton Key Basin, Windley Key, Lignumvitae Key, Duck Key, Boot Key, Big Pine Key, No Name Key, Middle Torch Key, Big Torch Key, Knockemdown Key, Cudjoe Key, Summerland Key, Sugar Loaf Key, Saddlebunch Keys, Big Coppitt Key, and Dredgers Key.

The names! The beautiful names!

We drive through canyons under stars. Headlights shining on a painted moon and I think John Wayne again.

And in Peru, just picture Winky ascending the pinnacle of Huayna Picchu. I wait for him at the entrance and imagine medics carrying his lifeless broken body strapped to a stretcher. The dark side of Agony. Then a grey-faced wild-eyed euphoric Winky soaking in sweat on the point of death appears triumphant.

I get so lonesome without you.

Together we drive the full length of New Zealand's south island. The last town is Bluff, southernmost extremity of The World. The triumph! Winky standing on Bluff Hill, on the rim of an extinct volcano as raging storms whip the ocean. I cry,

Come back. You can't go any further!

Remember struggling up a never-ending flight of stairs inside that timber building in Oxford? God my poor knees. Winky urging *come on*. Only to enter a huge bare room and Bliss shouting,

What the hell. There is nothing here!

Okay the view.

On the bus to Iguazu Falls, I show Winky my right arm slowly swelling to the size of a melon.

Something bit me.

Oh my god.

And the *fun* of battling our way through a million tourists to the outermost edge of the Falls.

They say, make new friends when you travel. Who says?

Stumbling soaking wet in the dead of winter behind the deafening torrents of Niagara Falls. I cannot forget the sound too close for comfort, the roaring walks with me, the roar my new friend.

Winky driving to the brink of ice-covered Lake Erie. Five hours without food or water and not stopping until he can go no further. He leaps out of the car. He slips and slides across the frozen waves to hyperreality. Always this search for the far-flung. So many odds and ends and Bliss yelling,

You can't go any further.

And after. The spectacle of Bliss attacking the 'all you can eat' buffet in the Niagara casino. Five helpings of prawns, cheesecake, roast beef, give me more more more, not a French fry in sight.

Montaigne advises, valuing observations and objects of speculation enriches the mind. Right. I agree, but Bliss the woman, she's not a thrill seeker. Terror and hunger do not appeal to me.

Bliss captures microcosms from startling appearances. Mind-boggling richness of landscape and nonsense. What I seize!

The primrose rays of a crescent moon.

In the madding crowd, queues, the endless queuing. That word 'Endless' crops up everywhere. We are constantly in queues. There is an art to queuing, to fill the hours, please observe people standing in queues.

A man with black whiskers growing on the edges of his ears. The man's fly undone exposing Disney boxers and the sound of thunder from his bottom.

A tour group wearing matching khaki t-shirts merge as a giant fungus, many arms and legs singing *who will tear us apart*, crawling through customs.

The semi-bald bloke, hair like lichen, the genuine pathos of a drug smuggler, the sniffer dog sniffs, Bingo! A cop taps pathetic on the shoulder, come with me sir.

A woman laughing, her mouth open so wide exposing elastic cartilage, the mucous membrane, the revolting epiglottis. Sick. Aghast at her fat animal tongue, we reach the end of the queue. And dead silence.

Until the sudden giggle. The titter. Tickets please.

Economy class, a battle of the human race. Winky takes the aisle seat. Damn. Why do I have to sit in the middle? Grit my teeth in preparation for thirty hours next to the man sitting in the window seat. He squirms and flaps bony joints taking up a discourteous amount of elbowroom. Elbow war begins. Fold my arms across my chest, biding my time. First move my elbow into five millimeters of vacant space. Surreptitious. Inch along the metal surface of the armrest. He reaches for a packet of pretzels. I nab the entire armrest. Hold fast. I read The Fortress Of Solitude. Flip a page. The creep repossesses my hard won two centimeters of elbow room. Fume. Wishing creep dead.

We the cattle passengers are at the mercy of a brittle cabin crew. They rattle past, pushing determined trolleys, clipping all physical protrusions. Ouch. And dole out wet rag meals, crackers and cream cheese, ice-cold bread rolls, a total of three lettuce leaves, a packet of salty nuts. What would you like? There are two choices, chicken or beef, burgundy or chardonnay, sparkling or still. Be still my beating heart.

More examples of contemptible passengers, mostly men, on international flights. A disheveled fellow who sniffs loud snotty snorts every four seconds for six hours from New York to Los Angeles. The wild-haired pill popper trapped in a Freudian nightmare, alternates between short deep sleeps, bouts of frantic fidgeting and manic conversation from Sydney to Bangkok. The bisexual, mid-forties, natters non-stop in a high grating voice how he broke up with his lover, moved back in with his parents, lost everything including a three thousand dollar gold chain ripped from his neck by a mugger on a bicycle.

Equip every plane with indoor plants in the cabin to absorb the toxins and the toxic habits of humans. I'm not being mean, just practical.

What is worse, the window or the aisle?

Aspects Of Arrival

Hunger. The decisions. Decide on a place to eat. Now all I can do is pray.

The male that is Winky, rolls his eyes the way men do at the dithering female not capable of making a decision. The male refuses to choose a restaurant for breakfast, lunch or dinner. He fears the consequences of failure. With a magnanimous gesture, Winky steps aside.

It's Your Choice.

In my defense, the responsibility of choosing where to eat proves horrendous in unfamiliar countries.

I will not admit to failing. Remember the astronauts.

Two tourists hit the low note, walk for miles and miles in towns, villages and cities. We pause outside suitable restaurants, bistros, brassieres, cafes and diners. We read menus chalked on blackboards and taped to windows and doors and balancing on polished brass stands. Waiters rush out waving more menus. Come inside! We have a wood fire, air conditioning, four stars, chef's special, fresh seafood, a set menu, hot coals, free glass of wine, no waiting, a buffet, a banquet, a rodent free environment, local delicacies like char-grilled sparrows, snake stew, soup made from a swallow's saliva. Repeat fifty times without stopping.

Confusion reigns. Cotton wool or spools of suffering grow inside my skull. I think I think I think. What blank this this this.

This disdain of hurry make up your mind. But I detest the restaurant interior, the staff appear hostile, the waitress chews bubble-gum, the spindly chairs seem precarious, the sticky tables, the carpet reeks of stale cigarettes, red wine, piss, oh my god check out the waiter picking his nose. Refuse to eat hamburgers, fries, intestines, blood sausage, testicles, guinea pig or tripe. Don't make me.

Next level hungry grumpy now. Legs hurt. Dying to pee. Craving a beer, Winky grumbles,

The pub across the road. Right now.

You mean?

I think, wrong. A pub beside a busy highway. What else can a highway be? We peer through the window, only two waitresses. The frazzle. Twenty people without dishes of food. We sit at a three-legged wobbly table, in the vicinity of a monstrous coffee machine, up against a wall, beside a column, next to the toilet and the kitchen, across from a group of heavy smokers, under a speaker blaring Iron Maiden Megadeath Poison Attack, next to a family with two, four, six squabbling screaming fidgeting filthy ketchup-smeared children climbing the walls, hanging from chandeliers and jumping off window ledges.

So kiss me and smile for me.

2

Kiss Me Smile For Me
(story)

Notes

The plane landed and a man put on his jacket and a moth flew out.

I'm leaving. On a jet plane. Bliss (Me) sings. Ohhh… Kiss me smile for me. Oops. And trips over. Ouch.

The pilot, assigned a holding pattern announces,

Sorry ladies and gentlemen, we are just going to fly around in circles until the plane runs out of fuel.

And the landing announcement.

We are close to the runway. Just not actually on the runway. But in a field near the runway.

Sometimes my ignorance sightsees too fast. You didn't visit Notre Dame? The actual magical canyons. Sacred shrines. Llamas here and there. Are you crazy?

Bliss of the quite unreal. Gets higher than the tripping. Jeezus my nipples go numb.

Let's go. Winky follows. Journeys within a journey within a journey. Waterfalls, ruins, saints, chiming bells, cathedrals, olive groves, Madonnas, mud huts. Fill brimming over oil and road. Away away. Almost.

First. The indeterminate state of departure. The soulless expanse of an air terminal. And complications checking in. What visa? We don't need a visa.

Flight QF 237 will be delayed for fifty hours. Helpless before the enameled smiles of airline staff.

Now sir, madam, we are doing the best we can to get you onto an earlier flight.

The inevitable missed connections.

That flight just left madam.

Wasted hours, airport lounges, trashy magazines, coffee jitters. Bliss drinks flutes of champagne. Oh, my god, the plane disappears. Well. It was there just a minute ago.

At the departure gate, a child ties a striped sweater around her waist. A vinyl backpack dangles from her shoulders. Her ponytail swings jaunty and confident and loud she counts down,

TEN NINE EIGHT SEVEN SIX FIVE FOUR THREE TWO.

With each number, she raises and lowers both arms like a bird in flight.

ONE!

She draws in a deep breath and shouts,

BLAST OFF. CRASH CRASH CRASH.

Every person waiting at the departure gate stops speaking mid-sentence.

A pale and trembling Bliss imagines the plane plummeting spinning nose to ground. The panic. Tell myself, nothing will happen. It's logical. Nothing happens in nothingness.

The captain, all pilots study and train for a hundred years to qualify in operating the dials, indicators, the rudder, pedals, stuff of every sleek monster hellbent for the sky. A pilot wears a sturdy cap. The many insignias pinned to his jacket. These must mean something.

Picture an A380 driven by winds, supported by air solid as compacted earth. Just think of squeezing a balloon, how the compressed air becomes hard as concrete. And the sky, well believe me, that's a sturdy ramp of dense stratosphere heading upwards, this gradient of air buoys the plane doesn't it.

Air is a condensed quantifiable body of *nothingness*. Nothingness takes over. Christ. Air is as solid as nothingness.

Bliss sits in the window seat. The window seems strange and adjustable, which a window on a plane should not be. Bliss perspires insignificant horrors talking metal fatigue and rupture and implosion.

Something is wrong with the window. It's not the right window. Not the sort of window I am used to. Should we tell someone?

Winky reaches over and knocks on the thick surface.

Nonsense. It's a normal window. Just calm down.

He opens his I Pad and Google's 'airplane windows.'

Shatterproof plexiglass suffers from crazing. Wow triple layered, will take a moderate beating. Ha ha. But my window has no scratches. It's perfectly clear. It's different. There aren't any layers.

A man in the seat behind begins a loud conversation describing his latest bonk.

Yeah Stacy, boy is she rough... yeah a grand fuck... and my friend Rhonda. Man oh man. Much. Rougher. Rhonda's thighs could snap a bull's cock in two. Bloody sluts. Sweet bitches. I mean fuckaduck what a night.

Buckled bodies stiffen. Not a Tiger Moth, this plane - but a real leaping tiger - taxis down the runway. Roars down the runway. Hurtles down the runway. The ground grips the plane, like Rhonda's thighs. The ground releases the plane. No. The tarmac hangs on. Heat and glue and bite this lofty lump of metal. Propellers whoosh. Landing gear retracts, crunch. Where is the flight plan? Somewhere. Over there. The air traffic control tower bends, its hair blown back by the force. And the air traffic controller crackles, pick up the pace. The beast drags the weight of itself. Get that thing in the air. Don't think about air.

I struggle for breath. So, kiss me smile for me, almost screaming, Fuck Bravery. My sweating palm reaches out. Smile *Smile*. Other hand, do I own another hand, white knuckled, fuses to the armrest. Engines bellow and snap at my fast beating heart. A thunderous noise scrapes my dry throat. The ground slides away. The plane rears on its hind legs. A stomach lurches, brain somersaults, damn this body to hell.

Don't smash into the clouds! Don't make the clouds mad! Those clouds might smack us around.

And what about the possibility of hijackers, engine failure, wings falling off, the pilot dropping dead, the windows imploding, the passengers self-combusting as momentum fails. How could I believe my own lies? Air has no substance. None. Remember The Ramp? What Ramp? That strong inclination in the sky. This giant path to heaven. A sensible sloping surface. Inclined to do what? To support the stupid plane from plunging into the ocean.

Jubilant jubilance of whatever of Winky. *Wow*. Twenty thousand kilometers. Bliss presses her feet against non-existent brakes.

Winky. You're freaking me out.

His fingers cover my shaking hands. The plane lifts them into limbo dissolving any past every future. All that remains. The here and now soaring. Bliss swears the pilot steers straight for the sun. But no, it banks to the right. Sunlight streams through. This flash magnifies momentary blindness. Light invades the mind. What if my head explodes? Will this liberate my? From that fear. Those engines roar, stop stop *stop* imagining explosions. Look out the window. Observe below the geometrical city, reduced to dots, squares, cubes and lines. The gods viewing skyscrapers poking up towards the sky and the faded moon asking how can human beings create all *this*. The plane skims the Sydney suburbs. A million red tiled roofs blinking a million sapphire swimming pools sparkling in a million backyards. And maybe a figure far below, watches the rushing jet, a microscopic reflection in this stranger's eyes, following the angle of its trajectory.

Bliss sighs. Steady in the sky. The cruising altitude. Invisible cabin pressure of insidious. A lethal environment of catastrophic disproportion. These peculiar effects on the brain. What if Bliss gets sucked into the stratosphere? Where are the oxygen masks? I unbuckle my safety belt. Cabin lights dim, the passengers unstiffen. Winky sleeps now deeper.

The airline magazine flips to the last page. A map of the world. Bliss imagines these countries alive and random shapes. New Zealand, a deformed turnip kissing the hem of a frayed dress, *love you*. The north island, an Edwardian woman with a bustle attached to my floor length gown. United Kingdom, a hairy puppy stuck on top of a Berkshire pig snorting, *what an inconvenience*. Ireland, just lettuce, its edges gnawed by bad-tempered geese. Scotland, a pregnant Hebrew priest. An impossibility. Oh, the USA, a majestic galleon growing trotters and a snout. Manhattan the legless anteater. And Uruguay, a puddle or an inkblot drifting on the sea. Italy, a high-heeled boot stuffed with foliage. Chile, a stream of melted wax. Argentina, a wig-wearing judge with triple chins. Peru, bait for a fly fisherman. Cuba, a cross between a metal detector and a hoover.

That's pretty good. Bliss relaxes. Gazes out the window. Ashen horizons of dusk touch part of the world. Bliss stares at the window itself. It definitely isn't toughened Plexiglas. And where is the rim? It's supposed to be plug-wedged into the fuselage structure. Sounds indestructible. My hand on the scratch free surface. Yes. One layer. Is it an escape hatch? I press the glass. It moves a fraction. As if burnt, I pull my hand away. The glass shifts. Like a sliding door, it disappears into a secret cavity. And there is silence. No deadly suction. No danger. Just a rush of loving air.

Courage. Bliss leans out the open window. China far below. This land the ragged shape of a chicken with the head of an old crone, a wart on the chin and a prominent nose under a sensible mobcap like a charlady's bonnet. China glimpses Bliss waving from the plane. Hurry. China wriggles. China of phenomenal strength wrenches itself as if a giant hand reaches from heaven and yanks the entire country from the earth. Bliss watches this spectacle. Such a deep hole left behind. Spectacular, astonishment, bug-eyes yet unafraid of China's great leap upwards. Tree roots dangle. Rocks catapult from soil. The mountains bounce beside furious swirling rivers. Houses, buildings undamaged remain at one with the land. The lights switch off. China rises taking Laos a three-dimensional form of a hen with only one leg and Cambodia the outline of a cloven foot. Balancing on this lone hoof, China kicks and gallops like a drunken concubine amongst the clouds. China gets closer and closer to the speeding plane.

Bliss spots zodiac symbols stamped on China's feathers. Year of the rooster prefers dreams to reality. China's old woman face now level with Bliss's nose wrinkling at my blistering breath. China the old ayi asks,

Have you ever visited me?

Well yes. With Winky on the ninth day of the eighth lunar month. Remember us? Among the leering porcelain dragons and paper lanterns punctured with unblinking eyes. And brass gongs clanging inside forgotten temples. The mist at dawn. The watercolor cherry blossoms. That yin and yan of upturned eves. China, the great rice basket, struggle sessions, ruin culture, ghost towns, polluted rivers. And such sadness. A population of faceless numbers. Unwanted baby girls thought of as spilt water.

The old ayi grunts an ancient proverb.

Be afraid only of standing still.

Okay.

China crumbles at the edges. Must go. Risk of revolution. And big complaining about disruption caused by becoming airborne.

The feathered land flattens. A slow descent, China returns to earth. To the black hole it once filled. Clouds of dust billow. China settles back with ease and dignity into the shape of itself.

Bliss rubs my eyes. The window slips into place exposing a dark starless sky. Winky mutters,

You all right?

Yes. I've been chatting to China.

Yeah? What did China have to say?

China says we have to go back sometime. But it's so crowded there.

It sure is.

The plane slides down the airy ramp. The runway rises - like China - to meet us. The landing thump, not too frightening. And Bliss distracted by an old Chinese man sitting near the galley. He pulls a jacket from his luggage and a moth flutters from the sleeve. A stowaway with powdery wings leaps into the unknown. This moth, not rattled by a child shouting blast off, crash, crash. A rebel moth on vacation planning to flit from resorts to lodges to cheap hotels with neon signs flashing three stars, Vacancy, free Wi-Fi, buffet breakfast, bravery and guts included.

Winky and Bliss exit the plane. The moth clings to my shoulder blades. Its wings grow larger and larger. These wings become my wings. I don't look like myself anymore. I move forward. I kiss Winky. I sing to him. So kiss me and smile for me.

A new trip begins. Lost in the brilliance of travel. Not looking back but stepping out of the frame. Easy walks around castles museums. Where black ravens, admire royal crowns, changing the guard, eating Yorkshire pudding and roast beef and drinking cream teas, warm ale, red red wine and riding red red buses. And in the future, the days months years, these memories flutter like a moth in the back of my mind.

3

Bliss Wonderful Upside Down

Notes

George Brain Lane. London guy clipping toe nails in the seat behind unemployed hedgehogs bramble jelly tea shoppes daffodils Japanese man with a tan wearing tails and playing the violin. Labor in Vain Hill, hit and run pheasants, dead swan in the middle of the road. Onion growing competition, Pewsy Road. Ball games are not allowed in the garden please use the deer park. Two Japanese Mennonite standing before a Lucien Freud painting of 'Sleeping by the Lion Carpet.' Man with an 11 year old girl looking at painting called 'Skinny Man' in Lucien Freud exhibition St Martins in The Field. Female violinists pausing, some rest their mouths on the top of the violin, some hold them to one size, indication of a sex life. The woman with the two chins playing the violin. If you are planning to eat sweets, please unwrap them now. A field of miniature white ponies, a car with eyelashes, pub called The Dog and Partridge, the natural history of British surface feeding ducks, river Ribble, Garstang, what will a wombat do? All the cows face the same way. London utterly quaffable, contender The Dog and Duck. Utterly moreish Dalwhinnie hot toddy, a fruity palate with a whiff of heather on the finish, a mellow after glow, Einstein on a bicycle, on the side of a red phone booth.

London, righty ho, evensong, royalism, rare books, death by alcohol, a white rose for Charlie. The mecklebugs, scumbugs and humbugs. The clipped pronunciation excruciation hoity toity. Ladies who dress with frills and flounces, bonnets like tinder boxes on their pretty heads and Winkle the dandy in his half-penny Macintosh, roaming streets paved with wood and a penny cigar dangles from his lips as we rush along grubby rain-swept alleys. This umbrella life. An old tweedy bloke asks us,

Why come to this miserable town?

It's grand, we reply. Ankle deep in a puddle.

This island, will it slide into the channel, no, hold your own, never be slaves Britannia ruling the waves.

These taxicabs, a hackney carriage mighty horses from Hackney transformed into black cabs.

Oi! The day I flag a sturdy cab and feel flaky and step inside, how easy is it to leap into a hack, but right at that moment, I forget where I'm staying and the cabbie asks,

Where to milady?

I can't remember.

Oh darlin, he moans.

The British never forget. The ordinary, the anonymous, keep calm and carry on, that Blitz remembers blackouts, starving poets in Wapping, in fact no bedlam as predicted by the toffs, bombings establish a sense of community, darts matches, gas masks, lucky charms. Tell me your bomb story.

Even the trees behave with propriety in Constable country.

Medievalism breeds enough fantasy, Lord of The, slap up English breakfast muffins, sausages, black pudding, mushrooms.

And twin beds for married couples.

Ah even so, how poetic lies the traveling life.

The pompous raving. The variety of smells. Not as in a particular fragrance of dawn and forests and the popcorn moon and the awakening sky, a touch pretentious. No, the real smells of tea brewing and Sunday roasts and horse dung.

Winkle and Bliss ride shotgun on the top level of a double decker bus driving at break-neck speed through Piccadilly Circus, Oxford Circus (Harrods lit up like a royal dowager) and rumbles to a stop outside Charring Cross Station. A Bliss and a Winkle disembark, become completely lost. In the throng. In the bloody rush hour.

The act of puzzlement, a man must scratch his forehead or in this case his bald patch.

Tell me again. Why are we searching for George Brain Lane?

A woman explaining reverts to rhyme.

I love the name. A lane named George Brain Lane. Lucky man to have his own lane and what's in a name? Everything. That's what.

George and his Brain, no middle name, easy to picture a bespectacled peppery mild-mannered nerd. Oh George are you pernickety? Do you turn your nose up at spicy food? Are you alive? Are you kind to strangers? You must have done something spectacular, what circumstances influenced the naming process of this lane to transform your identity, this signifier of some good deed, indeed. A car accident maybe, leaving you in a vegetative state, a coma, without brain activity as in extinct, unable to move your mouth or respond to questions, my many many questions, how a name proves a source of knowledge in human activities and cultural landscapes wherever. Hey after fifteen years you regain movement in your hand and with a series of taps, communicate a brilliant story of hope and patience and belief. You dream your life away. This brings tears. I wish we could find George Brain Lane, vital for knowledge of the past. Okay ask someone for directions. It's pointless. Londoners cower. Am I brandishing a meat cleaver?

Bugger. No one in this city has any idea where anything *is*. Consult online maps and Google directs us to The London Clinic, specialists in neurology. Should I ask a brain surgeon? Has *anyone* with a brain heard of George Brain Lane?

A colonial tiptoes through the mother country. Picture-book Bliss adjusting to London town of innate superiority, almighty blighty keeping the pound, the inches, the feet, the miles. The rules. What are the rules? Stiff your upper lip and apologize. For everything.

Own up to my identity. Colonial and introvert. Certain countries make an introvert behave differently. Subtle changes happen to an awkward soul, out of my comfort zone. The persistent feeling of feeling the feeling of being out of place. Self-conscious among the proper English grown-ups, the Saville-Row suits, the fob watches, the monocles. Try to fit in. *Gawd* that's bollocks. For an introvert disappears. My hair flattens, my face bloats and my Australian accent becomes pronounced, like a bogan from Toowoomba, displeasing to refined English ears. Oh God. Solution, stick an unlit pipe in my mouth and keep repeating, it's a lovely day. When quite clearly, it isn't.

Try to appear approachable. But the smile of an introvert becomes a scary fixed grin. I chatter nervously, begin unnecessary conversations, forced interactions, welcome let me be your friend, comrade, come dance in the rain, splash the puddles. Or be silent. An introvert becomes fluent in silence.

Mind the gap. No?

Walk away then. Miss out on my wonder, my not fitting into boxes, realizing it's surprising how many people do fit if you chop them to pieces.

Lean on the bar another pint of ale, holes in a dart board, steak and kidney pie at the pub, chat beside a real fire, a gas fire and outside it's so cold faces pucker and pinch, pull the plug, pull the other one.

Do not trust cranky horses. Outside Buckingham Palace, a sign warns. *Beware Horses May Kick or Bite! Thank You.*

Thank you Bliss, for your awareness. The British flaunt The Importance of Politeness. The orderly manner of queuing. Never skip to the front or jump the queue, resulting in either an obscure 'tut tut' or a riot.

Weasel Brit-speak, never complain, stiff upper lip, it's one of those things, comment, it's a lovely day, two hundred times a day, don't tell the truth, don't lie. Say everything, with the greatest respect. But all the while thinking, you are an idiot. I think that is a brave proposal (you are insane). Might I suggest? (do it or be prepared to justify yourself). Very interesting (flipping nonsense). I'll bear that in mind (I've forgotten it already). I am sure this is my fault (you are to blame). Say, I almost agree (I completely disagree). We could consider other options (I hate your idea). Quite good (pretty disappointing). Blimey. Just say what you think.

Take a stroll down Fleet Street, walk up a covered way and enter Ye Olde Cheshire Cheese and eat a good plain dinner and drink good wine. Ye old tavern, ex-brothel, oldy worldy pub surviving the reign of fifteen kings and queens, once home to Polly the parrot there must be a parrot now deceased, there must be the ghost of a bird and rumors! That a heap of bastard children's bones are buried under the floorboards and in the walls of keep warm on a cold winter's night and happy hauntings. The children's souls ride in carriages through the streets of London and pass us like a whiff of Yeats's poetic breath and it's bad, like rotten eggs.

Float a vision or a waking dream of life. The ritual of pretense, no, not an escape from reality, but a magnification of illusion. Choose imagination to dominate many minds. Do you mind? With more than one way to view actuality, create the possibility of laughter and a better life really. But who knows? What is possible and it's cold and dark by three in the afternoon.

Robin Hood, legend, rebel, an outlaw taking on the ruling class he frisks it over the plain, and chaunts a roundelay. Bliss be Maid Marion and Winkle my Friar Tuck. My merry man, the merry greenwood and merry leaves so green. Wine leads to this way of thinking until.

High tea laced with whiskey, hot toddy aspirations at The Orangery, formal gardens surround a stylish palace, tasteful Georgian architecture and crisp white tablecloths on every table oooh. The delusion of aristocracy, fancy airs, suppress a yawn, Christ never confuse elegance with snobbery, elevate pinkies and sip Orange Pekoe, fake poise nibbles an elegant assortment of cucumber sandwiches, orange-scented clotted cream, steamed ginger pudding, Cornish butter, Potted Gloucester Old Spot Pork, fruit cake, pickled rhubarb and spotted dick giggles at the idea of spots on a dick. Talk in a flutey voice,

Frightful, pleasing prospects, how vulgar, toodle-pip, hells bells, hurrah.

Will that be all Madam?

Bells on my fingers bells on my.

Cultivate passive arrogance. Dainty fingers and hair perfumed with orange blossom and skin like buttery cream and blushing lips the color of rhubarb. For we possess fabulous power, darling, yes we do, enabling us to establish reasons for continuing to believe what we want to believe, your royal highness. Do we deceive ourselves? Always.

The Orangery lacks mirrors, a convenient avoidance of seeing ourselves as we truly are, of shattering our royal dream, of Winkle scoffing the last currant scone. Crumbs cling to his cashmere sweater. Bliss spills tea on the tablecloth. A dollop of cream falls from Winkle's spoon into his lap. Hey clutzes, commoners, peasants, bumpkins, plebeians, the unwashed. The journey from obliviousness to problematic self-awareness. How can we be? Gallant knights, gay maidens, lovers die lovesick, the wives are shrews, the cuckolds are gullible. Give me the royal sword, a yeoman of virtue, Winkle the grinning Whig, the king and Bliss, a fickle queen, from a bonny blue cap to a silken hood.

We are courageous, loyal and cruel.

This bunglers' tirade, as heaven decrees, these flippant words command, thy flaming sword, the seas do swell with blood so don't speak with your mouth full! Mind your manners, pass the pork. I'm the boss. Are you thinking we are just goddamn tourists? Let them eat cake. Okay. Let us eat cake. And dover sole and let's hold hands and cross the next drawbridge over a moat and when is Queen Victoria's Jubilee.

Do we want to see ourselves as we truly are?

In the distance, hey ho a shipwreck, a galleon, a mountain of pirate's treasure, a silver object in Kensington Gardens. Mirrors in the park. A curving wall of reflecting steel in the shape of a C sideways, not quite reconnecting with itself, standing on a square of concrete. Anish Kapoor's sculpture installation C-Curve. Pontificate true to style, the outer surface a convex, mirroring the park right side up. The greens and blues of earth and sky safe in their correct locations. But the other side of the installation, the inner side, a distorted illusion. Introverted. The surface concave reflects an upside down landscape, reflects Bliss topsy-turvy standing on her head. You belong here. Light-headed balances on air, on skies, on clouds and above the suspended grass grips my boots. My body grows down with the trees, down to the sky, my shape the emblem of inversion. An image of the contrary. A lesson in perspective, drives me nuts, how we perceive, how we become aware. Wow Bliss looks wonderful upside down, empowered, more serious, dignified and impressive. A human gone the wrong way up. Blood rushing to my brain. Which doesn't happen often. Are you nodding?

St Martins-In-The-Fields, what whirls in, what I think, Domesday Book, Henry VIII big Medieval history of this church splendor. Of hexastyle portico and elegant steeple with ball and weathervane. Consider intercolumniations, a pedimented entablature, the Royal Arms crown and garter, carved on the tympanum. A frieze inscribed, D. SACRAM AEDEM: S. MARTINI PAROCHIANI EXTRUI FEC. A.D. MDC-CXXVI. Latin? Old English? Ribs form coffers carved with a guilloche. Yummy. Think ornate plinths, balustrades, parapets, pilasters, arches, cartouches, naves, cornices, cherubim's, this parish of bishops, priors, vicars, brethren, parochial dues, churchwardens, it is beauty and all that is beautiful peals a Sanctus bell from olden times.

Go down below for a comforting stew and a glass of wine deep in the subterranean brick and stone crypt where indigents once took a kip, its floor of ancient tombstones and a whipping post in one corner.

Ahh makes me weary.

At the concert upstairs, we rent a cushion for a quid, candles flicker warm lighting all civilization murmurs a symphonic prelude preparing us for the heaven of an orchestra playing Mozart and Handel by candlelight. Pews fill with a well-dressed audience, angel wings sprouting from spines as straight as church spires, busts on marble pedestals, these industrious Christians. Every puritan glows. So much that I feel fat and grubby and a dullard wallflower wishing for a pleated skirt and a silken pigtail and skin like a newborn peach.

I feel like a trespasser. A social outcast in a mass of civility. Caught between a gangster's whim and pure ideals. An outsider, the evolutionary reason goes back to the expulsion of early humans from a tribe means wild animal attack or starvation.

Stay gold, Bliss, you got the skeleton shirt, some of us just don't belong. The battle to be nobody but myself in this world of talent. Of musicians chatting quietly, their freshly shampooed mahogany hair shines and shines. A female violinist plucks a few strings, the violin balances on her knees, her mouth presses against the scroll thoughtful, anticipating. And the conductor struts out, chest puffing with pride like a peacock in a tux. He raises his baton to a collective intake of breath and we are lost in rich sounds, trills, sonorous bass transfixing young adults, taming children, everyone. We'll live enthralled forever as outsiders, soft candlelight lighting the way inside.

A contrast from that guy clipping his toenails on the bus and the punk kid riding the tube with his mouth open gobbling fish and chips wrapped in newspaper.

Why can't I just listen to the music?

Exit St-Martin-In-The-Fields and observe at the entrance, a sign requesting, *If you are planning to eat sweets please unwrap them now.* Sweet. The crackle of cellophane not compatible with a symphony and also annoying.

The masses shuffle, multitudes jostle through The National Portrait Gallery to view a Lucien Freud Retrospective brilliance. A backpack swipes me across the face, what the fuck, elbows jab my ears, shoulders bump me. An art enthusiast breathes heavily on the back of my neck. Garlic breath. Desperate darts around the rooms, in a search for gaps in the throng. Trip over a pram. Quiet please, make room, move on, don't hog the *majesty*, have you never heard of babysitters, stop pushing. I stand on the tippy toes of my murderous thoughts.

Two Japanese men, maybe Mennonites stand speechless before Sleeping By The Lion Carpet. This painting of a massive nude woman slumping in a chair. The foreground, wave upon wave of abundant flesh, of heaving and spilling fatness. A carpet, a woven image of two stalking lions hangs in the background. Kings of the jungle. Are the Mennonites repulsed, shocked, overwhelmed? Or do they sport lascivious expressions overtaken by desire? And a compulsion to hurl themselves at the nude's ample belly. Bury each other under the boulder-sized breasts. Suckle the giant nipples. Wrap skinny arms around knees the size of the moon. Does the lushness of unimaginable tactile pleasure enrapture, seduce and confront them with the temptation to succumb to a magnanimous suffocation? Death by flesh.

And it doesn't end here.

A professor lectures his young daughter, I hope she's his daughter, on Freud's painting of a naked man lying on his back, a whippet pressing against his thigh, his vermillion penis bulging at the girl's eyelevel. With one hand on his daughter's shoulder, the father lectures,

Now Clare, observe the model's skin tones. Pale, greyish and mellow. How Freud renders the face in a brick color. Notice how Freud cleverly foreshortens the physique.

Poor child balances on one leg. Her right foot kicks the back of her left ankle. Dreamy eyes look up at her father. Her expression bored by the rose madder dick, the hairy balls, the layers of flesh, the taut muscles. She tugs at her father's jacket,

I want an ice-cream. You promised.

A woman drags a toddler through the gallery. The child screaming,

I don't want to see no more stupid paintings.

I stay all day and take note of the occasional screams.

Ham, a quintessential village, we stay four weeks now. Chilly weather, on the threshold of spring, a host of clouds. Jaunty daffodils float on vales and dales. Historic village of narrow laneways and a single pub the Crown and Anchor. Hungry in Ham lets have lunch at the pub. But ye auld alehouse is a vegetarian restaurant. Can you believe it? In *Ham*.

Ham, faintly literary, famous for Ham Spray House owned by bisexual Lytton Strachey adored by the bohemian Dora Carrington, her ashes now buried under the laurels. And Strachey ruminating on his deathbed,

If this is dying, I don't think much of it.

Me neither.

Yew Tree Cottage, perfect name for a thatched house, its garden knee deep in snowdrops. A blush sitting room tasseled drapes gather atmosphere. Fall in love with this room, the sun reflecting a stream of dust, stains on the carpet and miniature tapestries of neatly stitched forget-me-nots and flushed little girls holding puppies. White doors, rosy velvet loveseats and plush satin armchairs in the corners. Bliss, the wan character in a Jane Austen novel, sits in this pinkness of supreme quiet. A comforting womb-like cocoon of peace imagining gentle spirits holding china teacups. Melancholy consumes this room, an ideal place to die. A serene death. An elegiac laudanum death.

Close my eyes. Inhale the scent of a single rose picked from the garden where a nervous pheasant lurks in the shrubbery.

Relax in the sun and write four words. I am in Ham.

Winkle hunches in this miniature cottage. He bumbles his way round the tiny dining room, the tiny kitchen. Horror.

It's the Giant of Land's End!

Thick carpet muffles his fussing in the kitchen. His energy, too modern and chaotic for long-gone centuries, the low ceilings and ghosts of Yew Tree Cottage. Every day Winkle bumps his head on the timber beams and yells,

Ow! Damn these blasted beams.

The valleys, the groves, the fields, the woods, the hills.

Winkle climbs Ham Hill. Shall I follow slower, collapse on a rock, this scruffy hill of mediocrity, the absence of exotic vegetation, not a mountain thank god, men and mountains, the masculine need to reach the summit, stick a flag into something, to conquer himself. Reach the top, survey the sloping chalk downlands, the steep banks. Come be my love you dear for the time it takes for the hill to jump into a lake, make a big splash, to peel an eel and till a fish sings in the fog.

I read the Ham Parish Newsletter featuring a short column written by Pippa Brackenborough, local woman who spent six weeks crisscrossing the Australian outback. The title of her piece.

Australia, A Peephole Into A Unique Place.

After a twenty-five hour flight, we sat buckled in our seats as an attendant sprays us with some unknown aerosol. If there is one lesson to learn from a visit to Australia it is the value of trees. The country is little more than scrub under a searing sun. What

a landscape! Barren, salt-encrusted, parched, flat, interminable and red. We rode the Indian Pacific from east to west and The Ghan from north to south and hour upon hour nothing but red flat land, uninhabited except for the occasional buzzard. We could hardly breathe for the heat and humidity. We met lizards, snakes and crocodiles. A friend suggested to me a visit to Australia was a 'no-brainer.' I do not think so.

Picture the fair Englishwoman wearing a Marks & Spencer blouse and white safari shorts exposing sunburnt legs, crouching in the shade of a single gum tree in the desert. No one warns her the Australian outback lacks fields of lavender. Poor Pippa. No one tells her about a big ruddy boulder smack in the middle of Australia, breaking the monotony. Did you find the rock Pippa?

Australia, a pushover, a breeze, no sweat. But breezes in the desert are rare. Sweating is copious. What is the opposite term for 'no-brainer?' No worries mate? Poor Pippa stuck in the never-never, the back O' Bourke, beyond the hypothetical Black Stump. Poor Pippa staring vacantly for hours at miles of blood red soil and at the end of the line a welcoming committee consisting of a blue-tongue lizard, a yellow-bellied snake and a man-eating crocodile. What exactly is no-brainer? I mean, *really.*

Bottle-green barges with crimson trim float on the river Dun running through the village of Hungerford. Motionless and flat-bottomed barges like aquatic plants painted on the water's surface and I swear they grow roots reaching down to the river's silty beds.

Name a yellow barge Mr. Badger. Tie a rope to an iron ring attached to the hull. Stack firewood, potted herbs and geraniums on the roof. A ruddy-face pokes his head through a porthole. Grins at Winkle and Bliss.

Oy! Where ye from?
A planet with purple lights.
Eh?

I hear garden parties. I hear musical evenings. We stroll through Kew Gardens. We picnic by the Thames. Pork pies, bread pudding and a thermos of tea. I hear a faraway piano playing the loneliest music.

Tutti Day, the Tuesday after Easter, a six hundred year old custom commemorating the granting of common land and fishing rights by kissing the damsels of the town, irrespective of age or beauty. Official 'Osculators' walk from house to house and knock on front doors along the Hungerford High Street. A yellow leaflet explains.

But it doesn't say if it's on the lips or the cheeks.
What are you talking about?
The kissing.
As if Winkle is supposed to know.
Look.
There's two outside the Hungerford Haberdashery.

Two Tutti men carry poles, decorated with streamers of lilac ribbons, tipped with bouquets of daffodils, primroses and tulips. And another man follows bearing a basket of oranges. The kissers work with enthusiasm all day, enjoying their duties. Lots of horn blowing, Auld Lang Syne and God Save The King sung with gusto. Falsetto shrieks show how nobly the Tutti men perform the task. As a consolation, all the kissed maids are presented with an orange. The Tutti-men retire to the Three Swans and drink 'ye ancient Plantagenet punch.' The constable's wife provides a macaroni supper and cheesecake. Which captivates Winkle.

Did they really eat cheesecake and macaroni in those days?

The town crier of Hungerford is outfitted in a grey coat with scarlet facings, brass buttons and a tall hat with a gold band. Lovely. He perambulates the streets and blows three notes on an ancient horn, then shouts Oyez Oyez Oyez all ye commoners... blah blah blah and so forth. He's a rent collector.

Some provincial Wiltshire terms no longer in use. *Thic and thuck*, this and that. *A Cadling fellow,* a wrangler. *Maggotty,* frisky, playful. *Clum me*, rough boisterous. *Dunch Dumplins*, dumplings boiled hard, eaten hot with butter and *Kitch,* congealed. And a thing is said to be *Limp* when it has lost its accustomed *Stiffness.* The British retain their accustomed stiffness. But we conserve a certain limpness.

Yet ramble on country rambles. For the love of hedges so huge they have hidden caves.

Mysteries of English rambles. The picture of Einstein riding a bicycle pasted on the side of a phone booth. Here and there, delphinine hot toddies. Unemployed hedgehogs. Bramble jelly. 'Labor-In-Vain' Hill. In 1780, a mad doctor carves a chalk horse into a hillside. Hit and run pheasants. A dead swan in the middle of a lane. The Onion Growing Competition held in Pewsy Road. The natural history of surface feeding ducks. A field of miniature white ponies. The River named Ribble Garstang. A sign in the grounds of a manor house: *Ball games are not allowed in the garden please use the deer park.* Of course we have a deer park doesn't everyone? Cows face the same direction in the paddocks of Inkpen and Buttermere. There might be more but I can't stop laughing.

Four peahens perching on a fence. Shades of brown plumage camouflages these peachicks less of a target for predators. Fat peafowls an extension of the fence. Frumpy fluffs neck feathers, caught in the middle. No fence to sit on between heaven and hell. Dowdy females do they strive for the moon ah no they must sit still on the fence and guard two cars parked in a driveway. So stay birds do your duty keep your pecker up. Not proud as a.

Outside a Hungerford tea shoppe, a Chinese busker plays 'The Last Kiss' on his clarinet. This misfit wears funeral clothes or is he dressed for success in his tuxedo with top hat and tails. Where oh where. Chinaman losing his china doll. Where oh where can my baby be. People hurry past him. Nobody stops. Nobody wants to lose love. No-one drops any coins into his paper cup. Which makes me sad and disturbed. At the same time.

Explore palaces, cathedrals, manor houses. Kitchens display wooden egg boxes, copper jelly molds, coffee grinders and the ever-present apple pie lonely as a cloud pretending to cool on a windowsill. I love the shopping list made of wood called Household Wants Indicator. Not 'needs' but 'wants'. We want what we want. Survival needs. Society demands. This household wants. All itemized in alphabetical order, triangle markers indicate such necessities as borax, chicory, curry dentifrice, dusters, and emery. Which are what? A mystery.

In the library of a haunted mansion. Who done it? With what and where? The opulence of deduction. Colonial Mustard with a lead pipe in the library. Does he notice the secretaire standing on skinny Shaker legs? An enormous quill to write with delicate pressure. A huge candlestick. Imagine a maiden, in her fussy gown. She writes her innermost longings by candlelight, of violins play sorry tunes writ with over-sized letters by the monster quill, come to me my love do not sulk, let me tie your cravat, light your cigarillos and polish your moonstones and together snuff out the candle. This fair maid born with laughter, dies laughing.

Everything makes sense if you give it some thought.

A dining room tables set with lace napkins and a plastic sponge cake, plastic Dundee loaf, plastic butter pats and plastic scones in a manor. Mind your manners.

And in another manor, a dining table laden with hand-knitted high tea. Tiers of braided cupcakes, a woolen cream swirl in the center. A four level satin sponge smeared with satin raspberry jam each layer surrounded by wool chocolate éclairs. Plates piled with unappetizing crocheted sandwiches. Fabric biscuits the size of flying saucers. Knitted pears, apples, bananas and strawberries, an illusion of warm pullovers for fruit. View this interwoven feast with my blank mind and peasant heritage. A card propped against a vase reads, *We hope you enjoy this very much. Take time to look but please don't touch.* Don't touch. Don't fondle. My hands itch. I reach out. Go on! Permit your fingers run wild. Buttery temptations scoff at the idea of knitted victuals. Oh desire, a forceful thing, this dying to squeeze every woolly inedible piece.

Inside the magnificent Salisbury Cathedral, daylight shines through an open doorway leading to a corridor. What light does well, creates playful ghosts, ambivalent spirits' fingers reaching for me, down the hallway. Break into a sprint, *don't run in the cathedral.* But the gesticulating, the perpetual lamentation, the space absorbs me. Standing on cold stone flagging. Lost in thought, in beams of light and burning bushes and flaming comets stick in my throat. Then the door slams taking the light and the pieces of my life.

A liar claims the stones in Avebury prove identical to boulders discovered on Mars. Huge rocks, lime colored moss, green ghost trees casting sharp shadows on the sides of hummocks. A beautiful. Word. Hummock. Don't you think? Hum or mock.

A day at the British Museum and I come away with images of tattered rags, horns, the black sweeping almond shape of an Egyptian eye, gold leaf hands, gold ribbons decorating a crushed head, a stone woman with chicken feet, no nipples and spherical breasts and a bony corpse lying in the fetal position, resembling an air-dried hind leg of a ham. The corpse's hand presses against a partial nose. Does it smell? No it's dead. I mean the actual stench of deadness. I guess not. Being so dehydrated. You know, I sleep in the same position as that corpse, the reason for my vivid dreams, since staying in Ham. Dreams of meat, so expensive in England. Ham on the brain.

A few awfuls, some horror. The ancient Savernake Forest lies on a Cretaceous chalk plateau, whatever that is, explains my shaky wobbles in this forest of isolation and spooks. Gnarled branches grab us. Dead leaves crackle underfoot. Glancing back wondering. What if a woodsman appears brandishing an axe? And I sense the presence of appalling things. The occurrence of bloody crimes. Covens, warlocks, killers. Grisly murders and bodies hidden in the dense woodland.

Nonsense, says Winkle striding ahead. I run to catch up. Something moves behind a thicket. The smoky head of a cow appears. I stumble over a rock.

Yikes a bull!

Winkle slows down.

It's a cow.

In agreement, the cow moos.

Breathless stops running and bends at the waist. From this angle, I see fungi growing in semi-circles shading small holes and archways in the trunk of a tree. Habitats for fairies and goblins gossiping on deck chairs in the shade of fungus canopies.

I have to pee. Winkle explodes.

What's wrong with you?

I'm normal. The average person has to pee. It's a physiological requirement.

I pee behind that prehistoric tree with a sign nailed to its trunk. 'Old Paunchy.' The relief.

I poke Winkle in the belly, old paunchy. Utter soulmates. That explains it. Utterly.

And how the British love the word 'utterly.' This idea utterly foolish but also utterly unique. An utterly quaffable contender. Utterly moreish, scrumptious, delectable. Utterly helpless. Utterly illiterate. Utterly ghastly. Utterly cherished. Utterly false. Utterly and disastrously wrong. Utterly reckless Winkle and Bliss becoming, staying, sipping cups and cups and cups of tea so utterly happy in Blighty.

We Are Lucky Enough

Notes

Ireland. Toll. Tag compare eFlow Betsy Shackleton in shaker village. Traffic calming, the term for speed bumps. Kildare: do you want to buy some cigarettes. Watering can in the cemetery. Old green and grey caravan with lace curtains. Pear and cinnamon jam. Beef tea: herbs and beef stock in a coffee plunger. Irish eyes are... Dubliners.

Seven drunken nights yippee *Fáilte go hÉireann*, Welcome to Ireland.

The Irish motto, We are lucky enough. But is enough, enough? If you're lucky enough, you're lucky. Enough a funny word, the final word, do I think luck is maybe not enough. Luck is random, fleeting am I a ponce to think this, not to pin hopes on some such luck, but to will, to know, to apply and get on with it, the search for the feast, take risks, never be satisfied, be lucky, be lucky enough, but is this enough?

The Irish term for speed bumps. Traffic Calming.

The Irish equip cemeteries with watering cans, so of course the flowers do not die.

Someone abandons an old pearly and peeling caravan in the middle of a field of tall grass and weeds and clots of clay soil, no trees. A bare landscape where horses once strained between shafts and furrow as the farmer clicked his tongue and worked the plough. Bliss glimpses the isolated home and thinks the definition of a mobile home, the shell of a snail physically bound to its shell a spiral pattern of nested rectangles the snail carries its home, like a car towing a caravan with ragged lace curtains and faded paint somehow survives looks like a decrepit mollusk wearing a pinafore and floppy bonnet.

Winky and Bliss drive tut tut tutting down the sub-zero coast from Dublin.

The town names begin with the word 'Kil.' Kill as in slaughter. Everywhere the Irish population huddles in nylon anoraks, too cold to bother murdering anyone. I meticulously count ninety-eight village names with the prefix 'Kil.' Kilbrittain. Understandable considering the troubles. Kilcock. Rooster mebbe maybe. Kilcar. Erratic drivers. Kilclooney. George? Kilrush. I relate to this concept. Kildare. A town killing dares, where death is considered unnatural, but pests must be eliminated. Kilworth. Speak for themselves. A dare is simply not worth the effort. Winky's eyes glaze over.

You misunderstand the true meaning of 'kil.' The word in Gaelic translates as woodland, churchyard or graveyard.

Oh so we're talkin' Gaelic now. Smarty pants.

We stop at Kildare and park the car in Priests Lane. Winky pfaffing about with the car keys. I wander into the town square, five star kebab, McHughs Pharmacy, Apache Pizza. I stop near a dirty dented Austin, its engine running, the windows steamed up. The passenger window rolls slowly down. A pale potato face appears. The reveal! A lifetime of stodge. The man all serious, expressionless, tilts his head to one side and lights a cigarette. He stares intently at me. His heavy brogue.

Would ye like to buy some cigarettes?

What? Err. No thank you.

Anticipating the Garda, he closes the window and disappears into smoke.

Church of the Oak, Carmelite Friary, Franciscan Abbey, mmm this battened down town, its inhabitants hiding from the bitter weather. Look over there! Where? One plain café open for business. A sparse laminated caff, a workers' caff, few patrons all Irish, all unsmiling. Will the coffee be good enough?

In a corner booth sit two fiftyish women bundled in green woolen coats and plump felt berets. They drink tea from the kind of mugs used at church socials. One woman glances in my direction. Both of us, probably the same age but she seems older in her queen mother outfit, brown nylon stockings and puffy pudding cheeks, her face like a freshly dug gourd. Me in my baseball cap, weathered jeans and casual jacket. Me, the strange fruit. The woman stares and stares at me. Her gaze, neither friendly nor unfriendly, more wistful, sorrowful, forbidding. Does she expect me to do something? Has Bliss broken an obscure commandment? Thou shalt not dare to wear inappropriate sports caps in Kildare.

The sharp day, wintertime, clockwise winding round The Ring Of Kerry, rings of cold, the unfamiliar soggy peat, a peat brain, lots of potato peeling goin' on, running water, this unfenced island of crusty bog, the flaggy shore, wild one-sided ocean of wow glitters the North Atlantic sea, an intense jade meets soaring rock face of a barren landscape. And somewhere inland a grave grows barley, a coalman sweettalks the rain and scones rise to the beeps of a future without clocks just wait two ticks. Catch the ferry from Portmagee to the shivering views on Valentia Island. Camera glued to my eye. Focus on fat blacklegged sheep nibbling grass, mortarless piles of holy monastic stones, forts bear earthquake scars. Bluster wind blows me sideways. My coat not thick enough. Gawd it's freezing in God's own country.

No toilets on Skellig. Help.

The picture on the website of this bed and breakfast depicts an historic post office. In reality, the place looks like an aged care facility. An ambiguous establishment of ornaments, ceramic floors, plastic placemats, pine furniture. Disappointment. Grit teeth. Bet the beds are fitted with rubber sheets.

The manager of the Bed and Breakfast swims towards us like a smooth salmon. Such a shiny woman. Coral skin and deep-sea eyes gleam. She wipes her hands on a linen tea towel. And printed on her floury apron, leprechauns practice cartwheels around four-leafed clovers.

Welcome to.

She dusts a bake-board with a goose's wing. The stove reddens, breakfast eight til' ten, scrambled eggs, white bread, no flavor in sight. A sign in the dining room, No Irish glass will be ever raised to toast the Queen. Right. But I like the Queen. Well the Irish don't.

Dinner down the road at the Fishermen's Bar. Crab claws, beer by an open fire, seared scallops drizzled with truffle honey, Ballinskelligs Bay sole on the bone and fresh from the oven, olive bread transports us to shamrock paradise.

A fisherman drinks alone, darker beer, a quick stout down the pub, snug as a gun, the Butler Arms hotel breadwinners sing The Wild Colonial Boy in his waders and peaked cap.

Ruddy-faced locals also wear peaked caps and hobnail boots. Avenge dear ones do not mourn. Glitter eyes sing Molly Malone, The Whistling Gypsy, The Rocky Road to Dublin Drunken. Winky sings with the sing-along off key closing time. Chairs on tables sweep the floor of peanut shells and gum wrappers and fallen songs.

Midnight of tipsy Winky and Bliss zigzag under chilly night skies, clear as coal, our breathless plumes in the frost, shivering, wend our way up the steep hill to our unhistorical lodgings, dull pine furniture be damned. Butter sinks under, the mud black buttery. A nuisance, tripping, falling and be-hind me Winky warbles,

The older the fiddle the sweeter the tune...

I jingle coins between finger and thumb and hum along. Shit!

Frights Winky wobbles to a halt. It's the smell of cattle dung. He sways backwards. Steady regains his balance without breaking rubs his cries, gurgles, passions. His pop-eyes bursting with wine.

Huh wassamatta?

No one gave us a bill. Not the bar or the restaurant. We haven't paid for our meal or the drinks. Do you hear me?

Catches our hearts off guard and blows us open. And we stagger back down the hill to pay the bill. And we sing so close to the music of what happens, singing the whole way, The Time Has Come, The Rare Old Times, Only Our Rivers Run Free.

Haggis Neeps Tatties

Notes

Haggis neeps and tatties, Robbie Burns, auld but not reekie. Puir Aulde Scotland bleat wi pride, a thorn in a' the wide world's side.

My heart's in the highlands. Just a wee drop! The juice Scotch bear aye good to fire the blood with rattling glee.

Auld Scotland chows her cud in souple scones and gusty sucker gravels round his blather wrench, Twists his gruntle and colic grips a Bliss slips poor plackless devil and Winky's gout torments inch by inch so what the cure? Love the cure. How easy can the barley-bree soothe and smooth a fumblin' dinsome clamour raise ye glasses lassies and laddies o whiskey punch clears the head, cheers the heart and strings the nerves.

My friend Declan, hoots,

Ha! Ye can see all of Scotland in a couple of hours.

A' the Scotts baith big and sma, that e'er the braith o' life did draw....

A day then in Scotland. And the towns seem modest, mean, ugly.

The caterwaul of bagpipes play strathspey and reels. Pipers incite mutiny and riots They sound like the asthmatic whine of a baboon.

The Scots once a race of savages, now a bunch of sanctimonious Methodists.

The Scots wear pleated tartan skirts exposing kneecaps. Wind catches the rebel tartan, a gruff ginger beard and covering something splendid, a leather sporran made from the skin of a badger or ermine or seal. And what can be a dirk at the waist with woolen garters, lace cuffs, a lace jabot and sliver buckles such savagery. The savage Scot pins a big brooch to a saffron shirt fastened with horn buttons. He tucks a dagger into oatmeal colored tights. And inscribed in Gaelic on the blade of this knife, *give me blood for I am thirsty...*

In the heat of battle, a Scot throws off the highland regimental kilt. He roars. A man in a kilt is a man and a half.

Scotland, land of the Stewarts my bloodthirsty ancestors, these fair-skinned freckled warriors, lassies, lairds, highlanders and lowlanders immigrated to Australia. Therefore the reason for my Scottish countenance. Bliss the Scot, aware now of my jawline's historic square shape. So blame a Scottish heritage for my short stature, freckles, stinginess and bad bad temper.

These offerings written in chalk on blackboards outside shops and restaurants in Edinburgh. *Haggis neeps and tatties. Rabbie Burns and Weelum Wallace. Auld but not reekie.*

In Scotland, they stuff sheep's stomachs with horror victuals. Braw bree, mutton black pudding, skirlie, oat farls, crowdie and clootie dumplings. Food, not suitable for the weak hearted.

A common thistle represents the national emblem of Scotland. *O that its prickles were a knife indeed...* This gothic thistle, a scaly serpent with a head of thorns topped with a violet crop of hair. *Plant, what are you then?* A beautiful and painful and reckless plant. *Your leafs mind me o the pipes lod drone – And are your purply tops. Are the pirly-wirly notes that gang staggerin oer them as they groan...*

Pirly-wirly.

We park the car on a sloping road beside Edinburgh Castle, a monument to killing. It takes hours to view turrets, soaring stone walls, suits of armor, shields, axes and swords.

A poster of a cartoon Scottish soldier carrying a duffle bag similar to a large black sausage. *Hey-Look Willie's off To Singapore with The Queen's Own Highlanders.* Willy looks about ten years old.

We walk back down the hill to the car. There is a fine tucked under the windscreen wiper. A pirly-wirly parking ticket. Furious Winky blinky.

Thirty pounds. Bloody hell.

4

Grandpa Helps The Magic

Notes

Santiago. Immigration man has hairy fingers. Jumble vegetables. Waiter asks for an Australian dollar. High altitude full of vaccination jet lagged wine. La Quenta is the bill. Alicia Villarreal artist. Asparagus. Tour in vin la mare. Tractor driving down the beach road. Mime artist. Tour guide. Our country our driver our lunch our garden clock. Laundromat is called a Lavenderia. Man peeing in the street.

Chugalug into South America midnight many moons ago Santiago sounds romantic, sounds like a song, if only. Do you love many moons? Do I? Too many moons means a life lost.

Twenty four hours on the road, in the air, low oxygen levels, vile meals, burps, farts, please don't cough on me. Two weary travelers, wait in an immigration queue for hours. That smell of resignation, the silent scream of impatience, the raw lighting, a germless atmosphere all packs a wallop.

One officer, just the *one,* behind a glass partition. Chubby creaky in a swivel chair. Round and round creak creak. Two minutes pass. Interminable burb bur burble where's the whisk the woosh the hurry. Creak creak thirty minutes to a brain shrivel. An hour of waiting. In the dream slow slower he rustles papers, passports and bam! Stamps his stamp. A resounding bang with relish.

The officer examines my passport photograph. He raises dark dewy eyes. Ooh shy his chocolate glances at woman drained of strength. The buttons on his shirt glint brass flash a smile. He instructs me to press my right thumb onto a digital scanning device and I do. The officer's expression becomes concerned.

Not hard enough.

His hairy hand covers my fingers. His warm skin. I hold my breath. He applies more pressure. Gently.

Winky and Bliss slouch into Chile.

The hotel in Santiago. Dark rooms with burgundy fabric and fawn plaid and chestnut furniture, creates somber thoughts, after midnight. Remember that song. The young me ago go, my first love, nineteen, a virgin strumming 'After Midnight' on his guitar by a campfire. Oh boy. I steal your. What a sop scene. *Fall in love.*

> *Oh boy.*
>> *We are going to find out.*
>>> *What It's All About.*

But no. We don't.

And wake early in Sunday in Santiago. Greetings breakfast buffet of Champagne and cactus. Cactus tastes like a sweeter crunchy version of cucumber with a slimy texture. Winky gags. We load our plates with ham and cheese.

Let it all hang out. Winky? Do you hear? We're gonna. Winky blinks at the maps, the brochures, are you sure. We will not be tourist rabbits hopping from surface to surface. Adamant no tours. Why not delve? Find the essence hey cause talk and suspicion. But not in Santiago. Do you want your throat cut?

A quick stroll, unprepared, jet-lagged, avoiding stray unwanted dogs owning harsh Santiago streets. Scruffy canines off the leash and without owners. The idea of freedom, the unwashed, the foragers, bone and skin. *Perros vagabundos* estimated number, two hundred and fifty thousand of no particular breed. Dispirited ghosts, curling head under tail, sleep deeply as if doped. The entitled sprawl beside rubbish bins. On the pavements. On grass in parks. In the sunniest spots. Two dogs wait at a stoplight. When the light changes to green, the dogs confidently cross the road with us and other pedestrians. One dog leaps aboard a bus. Tickets please. An irate shopkeeper, what shop, butcher baker candlestick maker, try to remember, well he wields a broom sweeping one sleepy dog into the gutter.

Do we need a rabies shot? Turn back.

Winky questions the hotel concierge about the homeless dogs. In impeccable English, the concierge replies,

Five hundred people bitten last year. Ouch. The city officials attempted to cull the stray dog population. Killed the dogs in a public space. Big disaster! A television crew filmed all the half-dead dogs lying about writhing in agony and broadcast the film that very night. Thousands of young kids got into a frenzy and make a big protest.

The concierge beams.

Such crazy times.

Prosecco chills in an ice bucket on his desk. He holds up the bottle.

Bubbles?

Along Avenida Alameda this extended ahh emptiness of deserted streets, of cast-off grey. And I realize every shop is closed, which saves money, welcome to an abandoned city. Bare wintry trees shudder, keep walking. Who wants to be here? To be like cramped handwriting loop-a-loop in a city of middling size, calcified and missing lights more hawk than pigeon. No one, that's who. The city speaks. Leave now. You are not big enough. Neither are you.

And listen over there, drum rhythms. A dozen Chileans drumming. Step in time. Rhythmic echoes totem drums, send a message loud louder. Come join us. More people appear banging their tin drums. Others with oversized kettledrums in tow. Colorful beanies and dreds and hippie vests and sneakers and tight jeans and pow pow enthusiastic pounding. This sort of beat gets our hips wiggling. Gets us grinning. Hammering ham and cheese wham pigskin whack metal. 'Gonna' such an ugly word. Shake your Tambourine. Gonna get better at. Gonna be peaches and cream. This banging city. Wild Santiago Sunday.

Graffiti covers the walls really swamping of color frenzy shriek impassioned tones of a plea, another language. Paint the severed head of a two-faced four-eyed cat Picasso-style and outline in thick black lines careful. Of course. The artist draws a top pair of shining human eyes and below another two parallel eyes. Bat those lashes pussycat. A speech bubble saying,

Whoah Whoah. Shall I sing What's New Pussycat?

Do you know the lyrics? I mean demeaning right. All my wishes. Cute little pussycatnose. You're so thrilling. Well I know. So. Don't whisper that guff in my ear. I hate that song. Yep the image of pussycat lips makes my stomach churn. Above the cathead a black marker scrawls,

Utopia Contra La Normalidad.

Utopia Against The Normal.
And down the side of the cat, in purple pen,
Arder.
?
Burn.
Huh okay. Set fire to the normal people.
We're safe.
So what's new pussycat?

What's for lunch, decisions decisions, the indecisive travelers, waver outside an ornate stone building Confitera Torres. Classic European cuisine. Open for business. Ole. Scarlet flag waving at hungry bull Winky pushes the double doors squeak open. The restaurant, the only patrons, an ancient couple bent over bowls of soup. Slurping not the best indication of what. The owner, a kind of quiet haze in a black suit, there is a smile, there is dust, there is a sort of supplication. He seats us at a crimson banquette under a magnificent chandelier a hundred blinding tulip-shaped globes. I search in my bag for sunglasses. A big-bellied waiter hands us the menu with a gravelly,

Hola madam, monsieur.

Hola.

Welcome to Confitera Torres. Allow me introduce Los Locos my selves your waiter for this day.

Los Locos with baby cheeks, dimples, round eyes, starch shirt, a tux with brass buttons pop pop, expresses determination to be happy and for us to be more than happy. He pats his belly, smacks his lips, innocent this sweetest smile and saunters off. Glory be. I read in the menu a brief history of the restaurant.

Our famous chef was borrowed by other housewives, family and friends. Reached such an extreme situation, the pattern, almost boring and not having his services, he decided putting on a business suit. Regular customer of this confectionery was President Arturo Fortunato Alessandri Palma. Account anecdotes that the presidential motorcade passed in front of the Towers and the President said, I'm thirsty pit, hang out with hot irons; ordered that he stopped his car and went to take a fishing chicha. In 2010 as from this date the sandwich President (Sebastian Pinera), consisting of salmon, cream cheese and arugula (type of lettuce) was baptized.

In Santiago, they baptize sandwiches.

What with?

Not sure.

Shall we try the Jumble Vegetables?

Good enough for Chile's finest intellectuals, writers, politicians and poets. But our final choice, ham and cheese. Los Locos rolls into view and gives us La Quenta.

Where you from?

Australia.

Ay giddy mite.

Los Locos asks us for an Australian dollar for his coin collection. I think, how nice. To collect coins. Winky looks dubious.

There, a sudden brightness on the corner, a supermarket lit by a million fluorescent lights like a Hopper painting. Stark. Shade my eyes and into this torturous atmosphere. My brain stunned by light wishes for whiskey. Stand for a minute. Shut my eyes. God, such a clean invasion. From dimness to agony. From despair to daggers of brilliance. Eyes water. Winky blinks. Am I being melodramatic? Again? My anxiety the phenomena the absence of freedom. Do they have dimmer switches in this country?

WING ME OVER THE SEA

The short aisles, the neat symmetric shelves, the low shelves for short people, the height at the level of my nose. Each shelf displays products arranged in a fascist formation, almost anal, but beautiful. Tins of tuna in meticulous rows of six across and eight high. Beside the tuna, an arrangement of sea green tins containing seafood, Isabel the brand name. Just Isabel. Next row, lines of mauve tins labeled K Ricko matching the tuna collection. Am I boring you? So turn a corner. Aisle number two. Rows upon rows of juice cartons, one litre, Necta Pina, Naranja, Durazno, Manzana. Oversized images illustrate the cartons. Succulent pineapples. Each pineapple looks like a pineapple and I think amphetamines and spikes. Oranges, of cardboard voluptuousness. An apple sliced through the middle, resembles female genitalia. Almost pornographic. And the peaches like buttocks. A surprise blunder. A sub-text. A subliminal development. A mockery. Sexually explicit juice cartons. Imagine a cunt on a carton. Ok don't.

Imagine a labyrinth. White honeycomb.

We swing into, I mean step into, I mean walk down aisle three. And it's homely with softer rows. Shelves of flour in paper bags. Hopeless and pudgy bags slumping against each other dry as ash. Again a coordinated color match. Greens on top, then blues and underneath orange and white checks. Pop Art but powdery. White flour escapes for the love of Andy Warhol. A corpse now.

Shall we buy bananas? Where can we find the tomato soup anything to avoid ham and cheese.

Second day. Ham and cheese for breakfast. We cannot go much longer on a diet of ham and cheese. I do not like them won't you like them here and there, I won't like them where and there, cheese and ham, I won't like them in a field,

I won't like them anywhere near and far. Regret not buying any bananas. The Last Supper, ham and cheese, a foreign land, dig below the surface, don't complain. There must be fruit somewhere in the city. Something green.

The sun today visiting Parque Bustamante, a free outing, a relief to escape the bland of a vacant city. Without a plan, just meander. Become a river flowing in this limitless park full of lovers. Couples sitting tight on benches, the clandestine kisses and many more locals here, a day out, ice-creams, ball games, why not it's a sunny day. A sculpture of a man on one knee, arms behind his head, under a big bowl. Another naked man in bronze, his mincing pose standing in the bowl and his left arm raised up, I think. We miss the usual bronze statue man on a leaping horse. Where are you going? On your leaping horse? How far into the distance?

Do you remember? The police presence in the park? Okay. Not that safe. But enjoy a walk, lovely to jog, to skate, to cycle the pathways. Sit on a garden seat. Listen to the traffic grumble any peace. Yet purple pansies and over there guitars and a cello busker's music tumbles sweet hats out for money and. A fountain, arcs of water like a man pissing. The continuous water arcs without rainbow colors.

Winky?

Yessss.

I need to pee.

Winky does that thing with his face. A slow simmer.

Christ. Not again.

We go into the park café. Contemporary surfaces, black and white tiled floor, a glass fronted gelato display, bistro style tables and huge windows looking over the green grassy and outside people sitting on beside a concrete pond. Inside the café,

Chilean families consume gelatos drenched in syrup topped with wafers and chopped nuts growing fat families fatter.

We are.

Hungry for fresh vegetables,

On my way out of the restroom, I notice a plate of grilled asparagus on the counter beside the entrance to the kitchen. Bells start ringing. Somewhere a bugle. A cheer. Winky and Bliss clutch each other. Greens.

A young waiter approaches us. A tentative boy, dazed, thin sylph-like, virtually translucent, his air of melancholy follows like a ghost. Pustules of acne cover his chin. I can't look. Focus on his eyes. His eyes blink, his eyelids on speed dial. As if the blinking contagious, I blink too. Not helpful. Feel like a twit. Fidget and blink. Winky whispers,

What's the matter with you?

Blink blink, I think Winky blinks too. Goads the poor waiter to blink faster. His hands shake. With eyes cast down, impossible to look directly at us, straight from poetry, his shoes of scuffed brown suede, nervous shoes. Without saying a word. He gives us the menu. Winky flips through, searching for the asparagus. Winky's forehead perspires. Pages and pages with pictures of sandwiches, cakes, ham and cheese. He turns to the waiter.

Do you have the grilled asparagus? We were hoping for asparagus.

The waiter's mouth drops open. A strange gurgle erupts in his throat. Winky becomes obsessed.

What about the asparagus?

The crumbling waiter shuffles backwards. His face turns the color of watermelon. Winky regales him.

Don't you have any asparagus? We saw asparagus being served. Where is the asparagus?

The poor waiter backs further away. Stutters incoherent English.

Haf no sparagush, sir.

I thump Winky's arm and wonder if jet lag is affecting his sense of reason.

Shhh. Don't worry about the asparagus.

But you saw asparagus. They must have asparagus.

Stuff a napkin into my mouth to suppress uncontrollable. Laughter. The veins on Winky's nose glow a fanatical purple. He attempts a friendly smile which appears crazed and menacing.

Listen young man, my friend wants asparagus.

Can we please order some asparagus? We saw a plate of asparagus on a tray over there.

Winky points at the espresso machine in the corner. The waiter scuttles into the kitchen. I kick Winky under the table.

For Christ sake, forget about the asparagus.

Ham and cheese for lunch and dreaming of asparagus, pyramids of oranges, legs of ham and slices of cheese chasing a bunch of broccoli.

I loathe tours, why, oh herding the gringos, the lack of control, the distant thunder, the grind, the closeness. Never do tours never do tours we never do tours.

Winky books a guided tour to Valparaiso, the UNESCO world heritage site. Only an hour from Santiago. Shouldn't take a moment. I don't believe it.

Are you whining again?

Shut up.

Kiss me.

A van picks us up from the hotel. The type of van that retrieves dead bodies. We squeeze into uncomfortable two vacant seats one at the back the other at the front for Winky the fatty. I smell car polish. Pessimism darkens the sky sitting in the last seat beside a wizened man his face contaminated by a skimpy moustache. His brown checked shirt and tan trousers blend and blur. Both his hands flat in between knees pressed tightly together. Are you afraid of something? He seems to shrink as he speaks. Australian. A whiff of sour breath.

Hello, I'm Ron from Harrietville. I'm doing the five hour tour of Valparaiso and you?

The ten hour.

Exasperation jealous of Winky sitting next to a deaf woman.

Heartless I am. Snob I am. Just plain unfriendly. I don't not want to chat with Ron from Harrietville. And where in God's name is Harrietville? Nod politely. Nod nod. Land of. Vague smile hi and gesture towards Winky, indicating I have a special friend and don't need another one. Open a book. Not looking forward to a bloody uncomfortable journey in this cramped bus. Are you, no, I am not complaining.

Ron starts talking. He doesn't stop.

The rotary sent me to Sao Paolo. I've been staying with a Brazilian family. Oh boy, can those Brazilians drink. Wow they sure can party. Every night we partied. They took me to all the local bars. After the five hour tour of Valparaiso, I'm flying to Easter Island from Santiago. It's a five hour flight. I haven't packed enough clothes. In Brazil, I had to do my washing by hand in a bucket every second day. Next year the Brazilians will come and stay with me in Harrietville. I hope the Brazilians won't be bored. There's not a lot to do in Harrietville. We don't drink much in Harrietville. It's a very very very quiet town. There's one pub, a general store and the museum. Everyone knows everyone. We're all in bed by half nine. There's a lot of nature in Harrietville, spring flowers, mountain streams, loads of trees. The Brazilians might enjoy watching autumn leaves fall from the trees. I know I do. Though if they arrive in November, I can take them to The Bluegrass Festival. They will appreciate that. Brazilians love to dance and sing. Wild they are. Then again, the Brazilians might enjoy Granny's Pantry. They bake such yummy cakes. Or I might get the Brazilians involved in The Handweavers and Spinners Guild…the Brazilians could learn to spin…now that's a fantastic idea.

My head spins. I begin praying. God help me get away from this boring, you're being mean, just listen, but its babble at me, the sounding board casting desperate looks at Winky, flutter my hands to get his attention, send brain messages, help! Feel free to interrupt! Winky ignores me. Bastido! You are doing this on purpose leaving me stuck next to oh now where. The mini-van swerves into a parking lot filled with several huge tourist coaches. The kind of buses I hate. Ron is booked on another tour. Ron says,

This is where I leave you.

I sense a tragic parting. Bliss absorbing the complete opposite sensation of unrequited love. Am I anti-South American taking such delight in escaping this enthusiastic companion? I cannot tell a lie, err.

Oh too bad. You take care now.

Then a flood of guilt, I am a monster, full of instant sympathy. Poor old devil, rather sweet, probably lonely traveling by himself and constantly having to wash all his clothes in a bucket.

The hateful coach of unavoidable. Sink into comfortable cushioned seats. Not so awful. Smile and hold hands. A beefy bloke slides into the seat in front of Winky and flips his seat back to within inches of Winky's nose.

Christ!

Don't fight it. Nobody cares. Calm down. This is going to be relaxing. I can tell.

The cliché of speaking too soon.

Five minutes, the final idyllic minutes along the highway yes strong heat outside and ordinary flat scenery of farmlands, sierras, bored cattle and an army of grapevines. But peace, any peace, never lasts.

A chinless man holding a microphone pops up at the front of the bus.

Hola. Permission to introduce myself as Gaspar your guide.

Swear to God. Hoarse man oh man. I flinch. And so it goes, so we go, glimpses of scenic plus talking invasion. Please cut off my ears. I envy that lucky deaf woman. My consent to exaggerate. Gaspar the guide talks, without drawing breath, for five freaking nonstop hours. Subjecting us, trapping us as long as the day. A perpetual equinox, what is that? I don't know, but it falls and we go on existing within this verbal marathon, a few lines of Spanish, followed by a stream of indecipherable English. Blah blah blah Gaspar expands his rhetoric on the 'what' and the 'where' of miles of featureless landscape. A few farm houses, more cows. Gaspar yak yak yakking and every noun he utters begins with 'our.' Our country, our bus, our driver, our lunch, our bathroom break, our garden clock. Our bus stops only once at a roadside toilet. Lordy lordy, a defeated anti-tourist gazes with longing at a stunning winery across the road. Stone pillars, rusted iron gates, symmetrical grape vines leading my thirsty eye, wine, we could be tasting vintages. Sob.

In Vina Del Mar, we leap off the bus and view 'our garden clock' amid much excitement, isn't it beautiful, the numbers are lilacs, the circle a hedge. Is that the right time? Bloody hell, we should be in Valparaiso by now. Our bus drives around and around the center of Vina Del Mar, past the Sheraton Mirama Hotel three times, sea views, relaxing location, atrocious customer service, one guest has a fly in his drink, no replacement offered and each time we pass the Sheraton, Gaspar points,

Here we have our Sheraton…

The excitement.

We reach Valparaiso, on the verge of our suicide. Can't be that bad, yes it is. Our coach speeds as fast as a prison escapee, straight through downtown our Valparaiso, the old seaport, the crowded filthy streets. Numb and slack jaw no longer hear Gaspar. Cocoon myself beside the dirty bus window. A glorious past, but don't ask about the military coup of '73. Just enjoy a green ocean, seagulls the size of eagles, a single sailboat in the distance painted on the sea, navy vessels sleeping in the harbor, flea market stalls of useless trinkets scatter the plaza. The bus hell bent but why now what for slow down hateful coach in a hurry. For no reason there is a reason. For everything.

Then as we speed, I see a giant man pissing in the street. His scarlet engorged penis, pink at the tip. An old woman holds the huge penis aiming an arc of urine at a rubbish bin. I cover my eyes. The image stamps itself a hearty sausage, sore, poking out of ragged shorts, the old crone her bending, her bony fingers lifting his enormous and the image grows larger and larger in the future fixed in my memory forever.

I feel sick.

Winky holds my hand.

You've got to get out more.

Gaspar bobs up. I wince.

Grrr.

Gaspar points at a gate. His elation.

Everyone quick! The gate. Valparaiso's famous poet, our Pablo Neruda lived right there. In that house with the high brick wall.

Pablo Neruda's house hides behind a brick wall what is the use. In telling us. Our sigh forever sighs as the bus hurtles past the poet's house. Tell me, right this isn't happening. Gaspar becomes sentimental and dreamy reciting in a high-pitched tone,

Ahhhhh Valparaiso how absurd you are…you haven't combed your hair, you've never had time to get dressed, life has always surprised you… Ahh ahhh few words, this poem completely captures our Valparaiso.

Gaspar puffs up his bantam chest and is silent for oh two seconds. Arghh poor Gaspar how absurd you are. How sickening I am. A frustrated, nasty murderous tourist. Am I strong enough to strangle Gaspar? Valpo, you piss in your streets. Lends the grubby town a certain edginess. And health issues. Winky the goodie always sees the bright side, consults the brochure describing Valparaiso as packed with a distinct bohemian vibe. Gritty and edgy, a faded beauty. His arm around my shoulder.

Like you my dear.

A Bliss sighs again. The bus wends its way up the steep *cerros* reaching the upper part of the city, crammed with shanties painted in faded colors. Winky looks out the window.

What a shithole. This can't be the UNESCO site.

I cross my legs. Oh God, I need to go to the loo. Winky frowns and the bus whimpers my despair. One and the same struggle.

In the historic quarter, the cityscape transforms into an explosion of graffiti. Let loose from the coach, the tour group charges through the winding stone-paved streets. We charge past Technicolor nineteenth century houses all painted in crazy candy-colored hues. Gaspar shouts,

Keep up! Stragglers will be left behind.

Winky and I trot past murals of giant green faces decorating brick walls. This fairyland toy town under a brilliant
sky. Vertical steps of rainbows and a realistic drawing of the
pope brandishing a placard, 'God Pot Head' and the witch
hat tower that make us want to pause and absorb this magical
Valparaiso. But we have to keep going. Gaspar seems driven
by some mysterious urgency. I stop to catch my breath for a
second, doubled up at the waist and discover an iron grill filled
with new shoots of basil. Gaspar pauses to point out a place
of particular interest. My aching bladder ducks into shops, all
refuse access to the toilets. In a café, the waiter scowls,

Restrooms for patrons only.

A furious Winky roars,

Give me an Espresso.

I scuttle down a corridor to the ladies room. And after,
we run the way people who can't run, run. Towards Gaspar's
figure far away waving the flag of Chile. We catch the funic-
ular down the hillside, to the sea and dingy bars and boats
and beige coffee and a frenzied Gaspar herding the tour group
onto a ferry under the cloudless and the sinking. Sun. I back
away, panting.

I refuse to go on that boat tour.

We order a couple of cappuccinos in a bar and the barman's mother rushes out to a café and brings back the nastiest
coffees in the whole world.

The two hour journey back to Santiago. Worn out sight-
seers. What the fuck, why the race back before dark? Remains of
the day, grime light, leaden magic. And my constant grumbling.

Ten wretched sodding hours. And less than an hour at the
UNESCO site. Thirty minutes running along cobblestones
and bickering and another twenty minutes searching for a restroom.

Oh come on. It wasn't that bad. Think of the colors.

Modern-day explorers, relentless seekers, conscientious travelers, wake up it's our last day in Santiago.

In the Plaza de Armas, we hear an orchestra playing. A Chilean organillero, barefoot and hairy, trousers too tight, the slow-baked chest, his arms grinding the organ for a thousand years refusing to sing those heartbreaks, oh hurdy gurdy man plays the saddest song in the world. 'Love Hurts.'

And always a magician perches on a portable stool. Plastic carnations sprout from a satin band encircling his topper. He wails 'seize the day' in Spanish. It's tricky thinking, here you are Mr. Magician performing tricks with playing cards before an invisible audience oh but the two of us stand to one side so as not to cast a shadow, this avoidance of being too in the moment as the magician shuffles his cards and holds up an ace of spades. Which means nothing. Winky humming 'Love Hurts.'

Mr. Magician pulls a series of dolls from a goblin cap. And it is easy to guess the dolls were in there the whole time. The trickery, not nearly as magical as that magician with a face like a nursery rhyme. He wears white gloves, a spotted waistcoat, a silver key chain clipped to the belt holding up high waisted pants and lying at his feet, an open battered suitcase in which a rubber figurine of Bugs Bunny stands all dressed up in a suit and bow tie. With paws on hips, the famous rabbit watches Winky and me watching Mr. Magician now motionless gazing across the plaza and all the while, we can hear that soulful tune, 'Love Hurts.' Yes it does.

For drums, cactus, peeing, two-faced cats, ham. Nothing is as simple as it is. And on the ground, beside the magic man, a placard leans against an old fold-up chair. This tattered sign says,

Ayude al abuelito magico. Grandpa Helps The Magic.

Yes he does.

The Museum Of Ham

Notes

Buenos. Twenty dollars for a pair of slippers. Number of chairs and tassels in the apartment. Drawer full of spare tassels and candles. Menu. Bread varieties, French, joss stick, Arab, figazzas, sacrament or big croissant. No soup on any menus. 'Peawns' with golf sauce. Plaza Asturias, thirty two page menu. Cut the crusts off the white sliced bread. Must boil pasta for seven to nine minutes. Man in truck driving down the road shouting through a megaphone. The number plate with silk ribbon tied to it. Leon and Cocina. Pharmacy with a drum for sale in the window. Jean the American woman at a dinner party. The armless man at Iguazu. Nineteen tassels attached to nineteen keys. Five men standing outside a jewelry store. The disappointment years.

Bliss the desperado catches a glimpse of her own ending. Searching for a non-existent safety belt in a taxi driven by a furtive and wild eyed man as if pursued by demons, speeding down Avenida Del Libertador, ten lanes wider than the Amazon River. Streets choke with out-of-control traffic, the gargles in stereo racing taxi summertime, murder time, a drive through Buenos Aires akin to Russian roulette. *Die gloriously!*

Jorge reinvents Buenos Aires as an endangered place at the trembling moment of dawn. How can we endure the trembling, the moment, the dawn here? Buenos Aires, a labyrinth of the vague, a sense of the indefinable. A mythical knife wielding ghosts and heroes, legendary tango dancers none of this tawdry yet. *all of it epic.*

With empanadas. Mushroom the best.

Jorge Luis Borges outlives the night. He thinks of a useless dawn and the proud waves of the dark *dark* knowing. I know! Something about the nocturnal sea of undulating molasses. Does he crack open a sense of humor or a bitter wave, anything laden with the unlikely and desirable, just think of him as horny in his own becoming. Jorge's thoughts turn to mysterious gifts and refusals. Ahh thwarted in love, he buys his lover a stuffed owl. She says what in hell is this for? He tells us such vagaries as things half-given away, objects half withheld. What things tell me and why half? You must read his, no I have not, does that make me overstuffed? Borges offers me his deep love for Buenos Aires. Listen. Walk the lean streets. Fondle his bronze ancestors riding vanished horses. He presents his insight, manliness, humor, non-existent loyalty. I find the untouched kernel of his self-enticing, creepy. Borges suggests explanations of me, theories of me, authentic and surprising details of me! Which I really *really* want to own. How I prong sensitivity. What if it's a load of shit? I find the bargain loneliness, the darkness, his hungry heart, I lost his heart. I plan to feed his heart. He intends to bribe me with uncertainty, danger, maybe defeat.

Welcome to Buenos Aires.

This city being a magnificent beast, its tentacles, endless roads spear out from the freeway. Imperious buildings line the longest straightest streets imaginable. An image of impenetrable.

And triumphant, motionless, an army of edifices, no end in sight, never reaching the beating heart of the city. Sad city where on these mud sodden flats by the side of a river, Buenos Aires, megalopolis, beguiling its whiles, the hustle of commerce, once the evidence of prosperity, teeming with successful businessmen drinking Cocoa Cola.

Cheer up Buenos sinking city how and wondering when. The coming fits of despair, a final summer, this final heat, of ruinous humidity and eeww thirty million fat rats run everywhere, eating everything. Oh my god, horror garbage.

This roast city of coffee and beef. Mmmm the aromas of dark roasting beans, meat on fire. Workers grilling meat over hot coals. Grillers right here on the streets!

Chin up Buenos, every day a new catastrophe. Rampant *asesinos,* watch out for *corruptos,* who could be *traidores,* for in Buenos nothing works, we cannot breath, we can't get away, we take a tranquillizer, lie in bed and moan about this exploding ham and cheese city.

Exhaust fumes exhausting us, roaming from café to café. These rich blends, infusing the people with a kind of shabbiness, weary from political propaganda, guerillas, escalating violence, twenty years of dictatorship. Where have you hidden the corpse of Eva?

Mate tea, the taste of Argentina, shred leaves into boiling water with a load of sugar. Take sips of Mate through a *bombilla* poking from a gourd. Gawd hit me sweet bitter. It's revolting. Do me wrong must be incorrect in the making.

Buenos conscious of its own qualities, a blend of. The keen. The alert. The successful. The ostentatious. The pagan people. It is forbidden for a man and a woman to take a walk together. Shocking. Is it true?

An underground railway honeycombs beneath the streets the rumble and Argentina, a stone universe changeable/unchangeable throbbing static. Will it swallow us? Shall we cope in this smoke city of wondrous, don't know what, but must be something under a sun goes missing or changes shape. No? A fixed sun set in concrete. With slight cracks.

Argentine superb and melancholic and raging and stale atmospheres and rotting decadence and prosperity grown shabby and the many grievances defacing monuments.

Too elegant for us, this upscale apartment second floor of a Parisian style building on Avenido Calleo (Cashayo) five lanes wide in Recoleta. A fortress of antique furniture and super bolts on the front and back doors and every door and cupboard fitted with ornate brass locks and keys from which hang tassels. Nineteen locks, nineteen brass keys, nineteen tassels. In a bureau drawer, I find a bunch of spare tassels and a dozen wax candles. It makes sense to stock up on tassels and candles. What actually are tassels for? I love them anyway.

We are advised to get some blue money from a Gambio, an unofficial money exchanger. The closest Gambio we find beside a travel agent on Posados. Is it safe? What if we get arrested? Go through an unmarked door. Three people follow us into a cell, chairs lined up against the walls, crowded now in the airless laden with guilt. No one sits down. Nobody looks at anybody. One man shuffles his feet. We seem to shuffle sideways Winky rings a buzzer. We go through a second door. Behind a counter, an obese woman, fungus hair, moles, urk. I avert my eyes, remember everyone has different standards. She snaps her dark expression, her dirty fingernails snatch our dollars, counts out the pesos and pushes them across the counter. It's a terrific pile. Winky re-counts them in the outer room. What an amazing rate. Rich here in Bueno, but nowhere else. Put them away. Someone will rob us.

What is it about men and money?

A man shouts into a megaphone from the back of a truck. This lone protest. The truck's number plate tied to the bumper bar with a silk ribbon. Nobody around but a few gypsies. No one listens. Too deranged, hard done by. Why shout so loud and wave your furious free hand and sweat bullets what *what*? We don't understand. Are you a representative of a political party like *everyone*? The man wears overalls. He yells louder, turning up the volume of the megaphone. Hoarseness creeps into his voice, this torrent, why don't you scream? Politics! Traitors! Assassins! Not again. Because here everything is. Maybe megaphone man shouts, Buenos is killing me.

In Italy, people sing opera on street corners. But we are not in Italy.

Buenos, a city fascinated by the possibility of its own collapse. Portenos the victims at the mercy of a city ruining each day. Fear of course, hide your bag, hang on to your purse, hey robbers on bicycles, arm yourself with cunning, prepare for long queues, mad protest marches, street rallies, demonstrations beware this city intends to kill.

So much pain on faces. Grudges hidden under a layer of skin. Layers of ill-treatment, tribulations, injustice. Women in pairs hurry past. Do they know something we don't know? Everything comes back to knowing and not knowing.

Everywhere observe the discontent, but we experience no riots.

A summer's day, the heat like slabs of hot meat covering us. Yes to the dress and my straw hat and solid sandals. Yet the Portenos, the people of the port that have no port, dress in warm coats and boots. Are they expecting a storm?

Watch out for bumps on the pavement. Plan as we trip without time or reason. Winky keen on the tourist spots, the tango, Teatro Colon, Plaza de Mayo, La Boca. Bliss not as keen.

On the side of the road, two or three gypsy women looking like deep fried birds guard black garbage bins the size of dumpsters. Desperation rifles through the refuse before it is collected. This terrifying greed searching for sustenance. Their restless eyes pierce us, follow us and we don't know where to go next.

A cruel choice to forget and have.

Lunch in a local bar. Avoid ham and cheese, dip into a charcuterie, refrain from indulging oh my lost Jamon. Order a slice of frittata. Bread? The names of bread varieties resemble erotica emanating poetic allusions. French Joss Stick, Figazzas, Sacrament, Big Croissant. In a corner booth, an old woman hunches like a child crawling from under a hedge and sucks wine through a straw. Her bouffant hair, a lacquered helmet as if lowered onto her scalp by a crane. Ready. Set. Go. Black dots stick to her face. Stop staring. Stop exaggerating. *Come on.* Poetic allusions? Allow me a few because the food is hideous.

People disappear, dirty wars and these memories haunt the remaining now free to express subversive ideas but do they? Instead many Portenos seek psycho-analysis. They cry, help us develop a robust personality to cope with life in Buenos. The answer, go back to the moment of birth and start again and keep a tight grip on your purse.

Winky and I explore the streets of Recoleta. Neoclassical palaces, art nouveau mansions, apartment blocks with lace iron balconies, iconic French windows, arches, grand staircases and pediments, this antique kingdom with heavy doorknockers on arching doorways and secret courtyards an affectation, the ostentatious show of wealth. Secrets must be the hidden places of shanties and towering slums bordering a monster city. And outside one noble entrance, the concierge delicately removes dog poo from the pavement.

The dogs! With a population of fifty thousand dogs, the wealthier districts of Buenos Aires employ qualified dog walkers who hold a specially trained certificate and a permit to walk up to twenty-five dogs. At. One. Time. There! Coming up the street. God almighty. Dog invasion. This seething mass. A pack of pedigree breeds, springer spaniels, poodles, beagles, pugs, dachshunds swept along by German Shepherds, prancing collies, bull dogs, Dobermans, Golden Retrievers and Labradors. One hundred and two legs, twenty-five heads, mouths open, tongues-hanging, panting, drooling, foaming, sniffing, grinning with sharp white fangs. Twenty-five furry bodies, stubby, elongated bodies, wiry, wire-haired, short-legged, some as big as miniature ponies, some spotted, sleek brown, shining black, curly cream, a clipped brushed throng encircling a man gripping a web of leashes one attached to each pooch. The lion-headed dog walker. His filthy windswept hair frames a crooked nose and tanned face creasing like a withered maple leaf. Under his bomber jacket, a logo printed on his T-shirt depicts the silhouette of a proud terrier and the letters Pablo Paseador de Perros. He strides with boundless energy, the leader of the gang, his pockets filled with liver treats. And the hairy flood dog/human collective moves as one entity conjuring a mythological being, nobler than all the gods propelled by a guardian angel. The dog walker, like a Roman Centurion, seizes the reigns and commands his chariot across the road, towards the park. Whoa! A moment of hysteria, as every dog swerves at the sight of a passing cat. Fire spurts from the custodian's eyeballs. With a howl, he flings back his mane. A torrent of Spanish urges the dogs. *Onwards ye hounds of heaven.*

Oh Lordy, supermarkets named Disco, Jumbo and Coto, names more suitable for a pet elephant. Inside Disco, a sense of weariness pervades. Miserable shoppers move sluggishly from aisle to aisle. Even the vegetables look tired. A limp bunch of spinach faints at the sight of prodding customers. Women drag trolleys piled with food, as if in preparation for a future famine. At the refrigerated counter of packaged bloody and dismembered animals leaking in disbelief. Beef? And this? Pork? Note the symbol of a pig in the corner of the label. But this? I hold up a blood-soaked packet. Not sure? Fatigue transforms into fear. God almighty, do you think it's horse meat or testicles or intestines or stomach lining? Winky, overcome with nausea, runs off in search of soy milk. He never finds any soy milk and searches for soy milk until the day before we leave Buenos Aires, he discovers soy milk in a market in Chinatown. Too late.

More despair at the checkout, the tailbacks, a shit-fight of queuing at each cashier. The supermarket stereo plays Don't Cry For Me Argentina, an attempt to calm the queue, but causing more agitation. The groaning of local ulcers, of resignation, tension, attacking packets of crisps, too much salt withers the Portenos into a fury of murmurs, the undertow, we can do nothing, nobody can fix this waiting waiting. Winky and I stand in line for forty minutes. Brain dead staring ahead.

We never go back to the supermarket. Why put ourselves through that?

Every day, all day, five men always in dark suits and ties loiter outside a jewelry store on Avenida Posados. Not the same men. Different men each day. Three of them slouch on the bonnets of parked cars. Two stand in the doorway and smoke. Security guards maybe, but why five? Gang warfare? The FBI? Secret police? Spies? Relatives of the store manager? Volunteers?

The shop around the corner sells handmade pasta. Behind the counter, the proprietor looks like a living corpse, a flour cloud wearing an apron. Not an ideal representation for the neat folded strands of fettucine, linguine and spaghetti. She hands me a box of lamb Ragu ravioli and waggles her bony fingers. Boil for seven to nine minutes exactly. Promise me madam. Precisely seven to nine minutes. I promise.

Women, stick-like figures dress in millionaire clothes, navy jackets with brass buttons and cream slacks with precise seams and bleached teased hair sprayed until set like burnt sugar, the brittle top of Crème Brule. Do you love the sound of toffee cracking?

Groups of students crowd the footpath. Ahh yes ripe raucous glee. From youthfulness springs a shared magic.

La Recoleta Cemetery, the many yesterdays. The entrance, a white palace, an atmosphere of peace, a sense of cleansing, of passing into. A labyrinth. Village of the dead. And marble and stone tombs the size of backyard sheds. Some in a state of disrepair, broken glass doors, coffins knocked from shelves, roofs caving in. These mausoleums cast a portentous shade. The resting bodies of poets, doctors, politicians, dictators, Eva. Somewhere a nineteen-year old girl buried alive, scratch marks still on the inside of her casket. This certainty of dust and dead for dignity no longer craves sleep or feels indifference. Find beauty in withered flowers. The glamor of souls mingling with other souls. And cobwebs cling to every tomb. Signs of life here. Spiders, tourists, pigeons. Speak in a low voice. Hush Winky, your voice is too loud for the dead.

Winky goes to Brazil to take a look at a dam for his work. Everyone tells him. He'll get robbed in Brazil.

Alone in the apartment, I lock the hallway, kitchen and bedroom doors and close the electronic shutters on every window. Don't over think fear. I'll be fine in this well-heeled neighborhood, a few steps from the Hyatt and Patio Bullrich. Reasonably safe until.

People start shouting on the street. Men run down Avenido Calleo. Horns blare. Cars swerve to the curb. A group of men grab a guy. Is it a military coup? Are they dissidents? Rebels? A return to barbaric traditions? Do they have guns? What if it's a revolution? The masses. The underprivileged from the outskirts invading the city. What if they close the airports? Kidnap me and shoot me. Les Miserable starts playing in stereo in my mind, a song of angry men. And from Avenido Calle, unbearable cries rise like blades slicing air. People gather near the shops. The possibility of inadvertent exposure to violence. Through the leaves of a tree, I see a huge man lying on the asphalt. Blood streams from a wound in his head. The men kick his prone body. Hide in the kitchen at the back of the apartment. What the hell? Text Winky. He replies, *Stay inside.* That's Obvious. Am terrified woman. The beating of my heart echoes somewhere I cannot think. Lower the shutters. Surreptitiously. Are shutters bullet proof? Tap the shutters. A hollow sound. Flimsy shutters. I creep into the dining room and open the balcony door. Take a furtive peek. Is the man dead? Five men punch the bleeding man. Don't look. Winky texting, *What's going on?* Two police cars arrive forty-five minutes after the attack. One policeman has thick grey hair tied in a ponytail like an advertising executive. He gives the injured man a swift kick. The other policemen whip out notepads and start taking notes. They appear bored. The injured man moans. Not dead, then. A man escorts an old lady and sits her in the chair near the curb. Text Winky, *It's a mugging not a war.* No shots fired. I notice a bicycle up-ended on the roadside. Possible ride-by pickpocket. Right. Vigilante. Traffic blocks Calleo. Footpaths and apartment balconies fill with spectators. As if expecting a street parade. An ambulance arrives. Nobody hurries. The moans fade. The man still bleeds from his scalp. Blood stains the road. Not the blood of martyrs watering the meadows. The rubberneckers chatting. A medic pulls a stretcher from the ambulance and sets it up beside the mugger. A young woman crosses the road. She holds a mobile phone outwards like a laser gun. The police ignore her. She crouches down, extends her hand under the stretcher and points the phone at the man. Her phone flashes.

El Museo De Arte Moderno in San Juan. Chilean collaborators Cristobel Leon and Joaquin Cocina create an installation Beauty and The Beast. The Belly of the Beast or The Beautiful Beast or La Bella Y La Bestia. Fuck that's a lot of uppercase letters. So speak these words with limitless passion. Spit them from lascivious lips. Horrific, the instability of reality.

The Wolf House, an animated film, the theme of how a person lives secret lives. Layered lives. Slippery lives where nothing in essence is what it appears. This elastic nature of myth, fairy tales and religion. A house continuously destroys and rebuilds itself. A woman is trapped inside the house. She is constructed of masking tape, cardboard, plaster, string all unraveling. Her desire to escape becomes part of the mundane world. What do you think? I think images of reaching for narratives of disfigurement, delusions, escape. We grapple metamorphosis overlapping tensions between desirability, exclusion, beauty and bestiality. I know. *I know* damn it. For darling Aristotle said, art is an imitation of an imitation of reality.

View the work. It's better to know nothing about the artist. Allow the aesthetic to invade the brain saying yes to invasion. Or research the history, visual language, nature and structure of the composition. Nope. Maybe. Discover expressive elements conveying the meaning. How these elements combine and integrate, the principles observed and applied in the integration of the elements. What are the physical properties? The size, shape, medium? Is the work representational or objective? What mode of representation is employed? Realism, idealization, abstraction, distortion or surrealism? Is the composition formal or informal? What does the artwork make *me* think about? Is the artist telling a story? What does the work reveal about the artist? What what *what*?

What if I picture my mind as a paint-by-numbers game? The numbered areas of my brain painted with specific knowledgeable colors manipulating my judgment. Will this make me think a certain way? No.

An exhibition by Sebastion Gordin at the Museo de Arte Moderno mmm a lamp base resembling half a biscuit balancing on a crumpled packet of something called a Jorgito, a chocolate cookie stuffed with caramel yum an Argentinian chocolate treat and according to the advertisement description, topped with a semi-sweet pastry bath. Unfathomable horror to bathe in pastry. Okay I cannot remember what the artwork is called. But the lamp is switched on. *Zing.* Forty watt.

Go from artwork to artwork.

Down the steps and into a space finding under glass a display of marquetry, varnished veneers of rosewood, laurel, teak, root of myrtle, maple, ash and jacaranda and what are the images a kind of trashy for each piece is a magazine cover. Cheap pulp but beautiful this new dimension of commercial transforming into objects of beauty and well it's been done before but not in this way so do it more.

And next, stage sets in miniature of football stadiums, Grand Rex, the Johnson Administration Building, place them all in desolation Architectural giants born to host crowds in big cities. Such fantasy, irony and nostalgia illuminate a realization. In life, certain insights become obscured by mundane events. The banal becomes blinding oh I really know but cannot think of examples, could be supermarket shelves, advertisements invading the brain until we blob about like marshmallows. And here this artwork resuscitates mush memories buried in a consciousness lulled by humdrum pastimes. Remember?

La La La I remember a David Bowie concert and me deciding without a doubt Mr. Bowie comes from another planet.

A blank brain grows curious and naïve, then slows and wanders the world, my thoughts receptive to an aesthetic of disquietude and the unexpected like a cartoon character skiing on the cover of Biznikki Nevado in the Museo de Arte Moderno, the description in English.

The work breaks through the gothic characters as follows cobra volume and reveals under the torn sheet the scene fantastic that right there says. Pinzaspala-spoon that give name, up train tracks, the train about to derail amid other pocket men fleeing in terror. Pop bricolage, the drawing 'reals' the deceptive game of scale. The implodes work gracefully contradictory metaphors. The giant robot that destroys cities in its path becomes harmless, almost tender, in the mini version that derailed a train Kinder egg. Everything is musical, everything is ready for the emergence of history.

This fear of derailment. Of course a drawing reals scale. Scale as a deceptive game. Scale and life. Aware of *literal thickness*. Mine. Own it. Be possessed. Ask yourself.

Why are two policemen dragging a snowman to a bonfire?

Well to me, it's obvious.

Because of the goulash invasion.

These diminutive worlds. This underlying play between outside and inside. Liminal spaces, in which nothing happens. Yet. The person, a disturbing presence, an unsolvable mystery, for *everything is fictional.* Right. Winky and Bliss on tiptoes. Everything. Fiction. Especially the goulash invasion.

Calle Defensa, a freaking long street paved with cobblestones and miles and miles of junk stalls and as usual, Winky and Bliss begin at the wrong end. Not surprising. This back-to-front on purpose a million times. It works. Not always. Do not worry. Be excited by spangle flags hanging from balconies, the art galleries, antique stores. Look. Crumbling baroque mansions belonging to the bourgeoisie, the threat of yellow fever forcing them to relocate to safer neighborhoods. Little moneybag men fleeing in terror. Ahh defensa decay. Some cracks and rubbling. Communist graffiti and murals of tango dancers covering walls of rundown courtyards. Images speak of seediness and vulgar refinement. Vendors tempt us, Madame madame mad man here *here.* A moth-eaten mink stole for a thousand pesos. Brass coins, crucifixes and faded postcards written with spidery script. Lost messages. *Having a great time wish you were here.*

Brush off the hawkers and hustlers and take a seat in an open-air café. Two tango dancers twirl one last time. Bow and bend and switch off the music. The disappointment. Winky dying to watch the tango and now it is over. A waiter hovers. Winky cranky because I can't decide. The waiter walks away. That waiter is picking his nose.

Enter a dodgy bar. Mmm, if in doubt order the soup. But I try the pizza. Greasy. Bloody mangled. How can we eat a murder scene? Give the waitress one hundred pesos or maybe a thousand pesos, not sure. Her perfect English,

This is the wrong amount. Far too much money.

She holds the note in front of my face and scolds me.

The money here all looks the same. You will lose a lot of money if you can't tell the difference between a ten and a hundred.

Keep walking along Defensa. Arghhh so many nice restaurants. We could have. But. Not to know. And no more random eating. We'll come back. Tomorrow is another day.

Six blocks to go where the avenues radiate diagonally from the Plaza De Mayo. Banners, billboards and protest signs line the edges. *Mama tenes Buenos pero descuidados y con muchas necesidade, Memoria verdad y reconocimiento.* Reminders of a dirty war. The forced disappearances. How many coup d'etat, mass demonstrations, riots, revolution. Mothers of the Plaza De Mayo, *desparecidos.* And the National Reorganization Process military dictatorship, unconstitutional, Full Stop law, Law of Due Obedience and the result. A plaza of the disappointment years.

Yes we are having fun. Are we having a love affair? Here. The tango instructions encapsulate an affair. Embrace. Forward Embellishment, Slum, Rough, Start Dragging, Sweep, Whip Repentant Candencia, Caress Crab Spoon Corkscrew, Polish Half-Moon, Kick Chop Pivot, Merry Dance, Trick Viper, Capsize Surrender. Which hurts.

Winky books a tourist tango show at El Viejo Almacen, a former hospital on the corner of San Telmo named after San Pedro Gonzalez Telmo, patron saint of sailors. Sail away some decay, well and good, the four page presentation booklet on what to expect on a tango tour. I don't care. I expect nothing.

The history of the tango on the back of the booklet.

In 1884, ether was used for the first time as an anesthetic for surgery. Immigrants arrived from all over the world and mixed with our 'crillos' and from that crossbreeding in the outskirts of the city, the tango was born. San Telmo remained loyal to its past. At El Viejo Almacen, we are eager to share with you our best tangos.

Ether, crossbreeding and eagerness. Can I just get drunk please da da.

Be wary. The price includes dinner. Of course an abysmal meal no memory of oh tasteless and fellow diners, the loud Spanish family wrestling a spoilt child, an immaculate Swiss couple and their two teenage sons, wearing smart clothes, wife with a blond bob, husband in designer glasses and white linen shirt. Bliss says we are just as cool. But in my heart I know. We are a mess.

Oh good news. The price includes wine. Raise our champagne wine whiskey glasses glug a determination to drink the cost of the ticket. Hold out my champagne glass for a refill. Another. And another. Blerg.

On the scrap of a stage stands a replica of the exterior of El Viejo Almacen lit with a violet spotlight makes my head spin. Out of nowhere, a Peruvian band materializes. Poncho-clad and dizzy pipes. The insistent strum of ukuleles. Drums beating rhythms to a happy death. Winky taps his foot. More cheerful than what is to come.

Taut dancers whirl onto the stage lit by a strobe. The dancers morph into a wary creature. Lewd. And the absence of love. Low-life hauntings, copulations, fucking, the tango unfolds. Step, pause, violins, flutes, the whine of harmonicas, the flicker of false eyelashes. She spins, kicking, slithering, slinking, gliding muscles, points and taps her tango shoes. Juan at her side, his gangster moustache assumes a brooding expression, greasy curls lollop across his forehead, hips flick dark and violent, a true Argentinian soul with the ramrod posture of an assassin. The kicking of their legs like portable ponies bucking and swishing their tails. Giddy up. Juan's unrequited love slides up her thigh, his fingers leap closer and closer to her crotch. Winky's mouth drops open, along with the rest of the audience.

This music of misery aches love, death, loss, longing from within oh for God's sake, be miserable, pout tragedy, forever turn and turn mmm the pleasure of pain, do not speak, don't make eye contact, wallow in your own unique torment.

After the show, the Swiss couple's two sons ask us to join them for a drink. The boys make introductions, offload their parents and head for the nightclubs. Oh my god in heaven blah blur Winky and I shitfaced in this strange bar with a straitlaced Swiss lawyer and his polite wife and me babbling like a trapped chimp, do they succumb to impoliteness and disentangle themselves from the Bliss the piss head, the disgracefully hammered, sick and tired of my blather boring them to tears, stop repeating yourself, please don't vomit, perfection eludes us drowning in wine, do you love to tango. Neither Winky or I remember how we manage to get back to the apartment.

Palermo, the barrio of carefree poverty. These risky streets, a gringa misery neighborhood. The avenues and lanes oozing the blood of a colonial slaughterhouse. As usual Winky and a nervous Bliss blunder about at Plaza Italia, we cross Avenida Santa Fe, my terror of ride-by muggers subsides but still we walk as one entity me clutching Winky's arm, tucking my bag between our hips, the strap across my shoulder so careful streetwise in the deserted streets we wonder where are all the cool shops, the milonga, the patios, the guitars, the radiant flowers, the bars and the bands playing. Nowhere to be found.

Shop names with rhythm. Ay Not Dead. Calma Chicha. Prune. Sexy Hexy Magica.

Keep walking. Okay Sexy Hexy has another underwear shop. A kind of grotesque eroticism. No name on the window, dusty with flesh-colored displays of pointy cone cup brassieres will this help the sagging women with hour-glass shapes wearing bullet bras made to lift and point the bosom and good luck satin corsets, boned bodices and pantaloons wrestle the indulgences, tighter, breathe in madam, create exaggerated curves giving an artificial air of speculation. As To What Lies Beneath. And elastic suspenders, snap, fasten serious girdles with hooks and eyes, nylon petticoats and waist-high cotton knickers designed for a woman to be squeezed into during an era of unlimited birth rates.

My goosebumps sense this absence of prudery.

And I there stand in my canvas Sketchers without socks. Bra straps slipping over my shoulders and the elastic in my underpants stretched beyond comprehension, relying on my trousers to hold everything in its place, aware my underwear fails to project any mysterious allure. A chill in the barefoot air outside Magica so in we go, just fitting into the narrow space between the counter and the wall, the only customers accosted with a more riotous display of unmentionables. Lacy slips with hems designed to be exposed. Cotton singlets of a certain practicality. Prosaic underpants favoring the utilitarian rather than the erotic. Hello short beefy man beaming behind the counter. His pudding head, rheumy eyes, a dirty moustache and fat fingers looks more like a bookie or an undersized bouncer, than the proprietor of an undergarment store. He waits expectantly facing rows of cardboard boxes filled with neatly folded merchandise packaged in cellophane. Numbered codes mark each box. Winky, delighted to practice his Spanish, garbles at the man.

Nos gustaria comprar unos sujetadores tobillos negros, pues no, quiero decir calcetines negros?

The man does not understand. Winky points to the pair of socks fitted onto a mannequin's foot in the store window.

Ahhh, excitement. The man rifles through the cardboard boxes. Ten minutes then. Bingo. He pulls out a pair of beige socks. No. I want black ankle socks. Winky starts sorting through various boxes. Two women enter the store. With suspicious expressions, they watch Winky rummaging through the contents of a carton. Then the women *push in* and start questioning the harassed proprietor. Happy to flirt, he abandons the search for socks. Winky gestures determined to buy socks.

Hola hola senor! Socks. Black Socks.

A lady, maybe his wife, steams in like a toy locomotive rattling copious jewelry and she lets loose a shriek in Spanish. Boom. He throws up his hands in defeat. We exit the store. Sockless.

How quibbling transforms into an exploit bursting from obscure circumstances.

Further down the road, a hulking man heads toward us. His boulder face and flame eyes, does he mean to kill us. Not wishing to face a violent death, I steer Winky in the opposite direction and as we escape away skulk at a trot, I hear the potential killer whistling fragments of a milonga.

Turn into a street named after the literature of eternity. Realm of the immortals, Palermo the avenue we fail to find. The pathway we never step on. What the facades hide. Here artful arrangements of fruits and vegetables. The sock store, a tobacconist, a cafe barred and forbidding at midday, to early, for the barrio comes alive late at night to capture the when dreams and after midnight, Palermo slips away from the present, do not stay late, avoid the remote more squalid era echoing lost things. Shadows without substance. Men immortalized in the lyrics of the milonga. These songs integral to the myth of Buenos Aires trickle into the barrios from the outskirts of a city built from fear. What I do not recognize, cannot touch me. What becomes lost, never belongs to me.

In Chinatown, buying hair conditioner from a pharmacy with a complete drum kit in the front window. Drums for sale. No price tag. Ummm. Wonder. Why sell drums in a ta dum de dum pharmacy.

The Natural Sciences Museum. I take twenty-eight photographs of a taxidermy bird display. I photograph stuffed and drowning organisms floating in fluid inside jars. This museum exists because a Dominican order expelled a monk. Don't ask.

The Gran Cafe Tortoni. Second oldest café in the world there you go old (*Viejo*) Tortoni, trickles the box of memories, this longstanding cafe once a refuge, a temple for intellectuals, literati, musicians, political outcasts. Now a tourist trap. Lengthy queuing annihilates the relaxed bohemian vibe. But still. Winky and Bliss bug-eyed, footsore, queue for half an hour until an elf greets us at the door hung with crimson velvet. The elf condescends, allows us, waves us through okay, enter the famous Gran Cafe Tortoni. Sit at a marble table, unwiped, the remains of crumbs, sugar and coffee rings and nearby the haunting wax figure of Borges, his magic remains the same, but for la de dah, a bland menu, chocolate churros, meat, chicken, the same ever the same and plenty of rude waiters, old guys hating every camera-snapping tourist. *Quick take a picture.* Flash. Shoot. Snap. Stay for a while, don't call us tourists soaking up the historic ambience, the wood paneled interior, object de art, art deco stained glass ceiling takes us to another world, so we leave without eating or drinking or saying goodbye and we go on to be millions.

Avenida De Mayo at lunchtime, lurking outside Plaza Asturias, this ancient dinosaur, a tired restaurant looks interesting, *no* not random, be brave. Legs of cured ham hang from the rafters. A waitress pours us glasses of complimentary sherry and plops a bowl of olives on the grubby tablecloth love this place with its whopping menu, thirty-two pages, complete with history and introduction translated into English.

As descendants of Spanish, we love as our merge two customs as good food and good service in a place where service and quality of our recipes prioritize. Our spacious kitchen allows us to entangle Argentinas tasty meat with the excellent fruits of Spanish sea and varied recipes, culminating in an extensive menu, accompanied by a staff of experienced and trajectory.

Urk. Peawns with golf sauce. Splash of white bird. Tuna spatter. Rabas to roman. Rice to cuba. Roman brains garnished. Ham riding. Supreme jockey club. The old woman carre. Peas mattress. Bananas burned to rhum. Torpedo cup. Surcharge of charlotte. Anise monkey. Difficult to decide I am. Woozy thanking God in his heaven for sherry, drain the glass and order sangria. The waitress sets up a table next to ours, fills a glass pitcher with ice and slices of lemons, mulls everything with a wooden spoon, pours a carafe of claret into the jug, just to brighten the afternoon. A mound of Russian salad drenched in mayonnaise by the window. Ceramic bowls of paella steam past us and this smattering of phrases, a British accent,

Too many beards on the mussel shells. The ham tastes like spam. Those old yellow peas with too much octopus and blah prawns. All leftovers. Never again.

Sangria often goes to my head. Slur. Shirty tourists. Whinging Poms old yella peas oh sweet Jesus you can never have too much octopus. The waitress brings me a dish of pork stew sweet. And then the entire staff sits down at a communal table for their own lunch. Winky waits with ravenous eyes. Watches me eating. Stop staring. Have some of mine. Go over and interrupt their lunch. He waits thirty minutes for his grilled fish. Annoying, I know.

Whizz through an exhibition at MALBA. Seen it all before. Nothing new under the sun. Artworks of clothes pegs. Right been there. Some spidery ink drawings on graph paper. Lurk. Molecules etched on Perspex clipped with paper clips, spiders in pretty bottles, sea sponges, paperbacks balanced at angles on shelves screwed to the wall. Imagine. Hang on. This poster pinned to the wall. The mission statement proves more interesting. Catchy title. The Opposite Of Magic. That can't be nice, but still I love it.

Explosive illumination is not the only form of knowledge and impatience not the only way to approach extraction. In Latin America, the life of a well-known scientist is often even worse than the life of a failed artist. How painful to go through everything Van Gogh went through. But would you really prefer the problems of the potato eaters? Huh. Potato eaters? And then a warning.

These are complex times and the temptation to be crude or dim-witted is boundless. Magic, which in the past has helped us to advance, will not help us in the future. What will we do without magic?

On Calle Florida hectic ow battle through throngs of shoppers, touts, shadowy characters, pickpockets and street performers tangoing, a swarthy man and a woman with a bottom the size of a boulder, short vinyl dress, high heels and black socks twist like a fat insect as rat-faced gypsy women balance on their haunches, their toddlers roaming about with nothing but runny noses. Winky and Bliss of hot weary bones searching for Somewhere quiet far from the madding and at the end of the street arrive in hell no approach what helpless on the curb of Avenida 9 de Julio, the widest street, longest pedestrian crossing in the world, an epic fourteen lanes, a wilderness of cars, buses, taxis, trucks screeching brakes, rumbling, fumes. Traffic revs at the stop lights. Pedestrians scurry to the other side. Imagine Moses parting the Red Sea. My shattered brain races with biblical images. Let us flee. The Angel of God behind us. A pillar of cloud in the middle. Moses stretching his hand across the sea of vehicles. How many green lights does it take to cross Avenida 9 de Julio? Shit. The walk sign flickers on. Go. What the fuck. We'll be killed. We flee for our lives across this zebra striped land in parting sea. Four crossings. Four light changes. Stop. Go. Stop. Go. Go for God's sake. *Go.*

On the other side of hell, an obelisk, a pronounced pointy thing, a stark homage to erections, skewers the sky. Why.

I am shitfaced again. At a dinner party, our hosts, Trevor gay hairdresser from Sydney and Jake, a soldier from Montenegro. I remember laser lights in the loungeroom. Bliss dancing with a bull dog, loving the bulldog, threatening to kidnap the bulldog. Mumble sway. And Jean, an American woman no not Jeeeen, but Jaaahhn like juuunkie. We never hear from Tony and Nino again. My fault. Who cares?

We never find. The Cathedral of Sandwiches, a brutal place where they cut off the crusts of every slice white of bread. Sandwiches as if without overcoats. This naked lunch.

Pork the true object of worship. Pork a culinary heritage at the Museo de Jamon. The Museum of Ham, linking the past, present and future. The Art Of Ham. The art of the distinct process of salting and curing meat from murdered piglets, exclusively fed on breast milk. If only they weren't so tender.

Here waterfalling at Iguazu Falls, 'big water' because an angry god (aren't they all) split the land creating a gorge and the waterfall. Goodbye every day, a rainbow born of mist and water droplets appear above or behind Iguazu Falls. Size matters. The broader the droplet, the more saturated the hues. Cloudbow, Fogbow, the rare Moonbow, Glassbows, Dewbows, High and Lowbows somewhere over the falls.

This shabby hotel room (but it's the Sheraton). The toilet blocks up. Bliss runs down three flights of stairs to use the restroom in the lobby. Don't go chasin' waterfalls...moving too fast...I know you're gonna have it your way or nothing at all.

Winky straps himself to the seat of a speedboat stuffed like a turkey with tourist daredevils and zips under the falls, through currents, whirlpools and life-threatening rocks. I watch from a distance. He returns wet through.

You're wet through.

Wait for thirty-minutes in a queue at a train station for the rainforest ecological train to take us to Devil's Throat. A pintsized train pulls into the station. We board the carriages. Squeeze us in. Eight seats per carriage, four on each side of thirty-five carriages fitting three hundred people, the same amount as the number of water falls. Chugs away. Who's counting. Just don't go off the rails. Be quiet.

At Devil's Throat remember the name but not the why and we walk across the falls, cripes this walking on water on a crowded elevated walkway. Ten thousand grim-looking people hobble and slouch in both directions. All refuse to give way, limiting progress. A man passes us on the path. He's wearing a green t-shirt with empty sleeves, swinging. Why wear a long sleeve shirt if you have no arms. Maybe remove the sleeves. Sew the holes together. Become a walking torso. But that makes being armless more obvious.

So much deformity in South America. So many cripples. Remember arriving at the airport in Buenos Aires? All those disabled people, hordes of them wearing uniforms of some kind. Maybe it's the law, enforcing matching outfits as a way to make the disabled feel to be part of a group and not isolated. Winky raises his eyebrows.

Those 'cripples,' you so merrily refer to, are Paralympians traveling to Chile for the Para-South American Games.

How To Watch A Waterfall. Teeter on the brink. With drenching body and a mind on fire. Eyes follow the white water rushing over precipices. Water, uncontained downward moving to the lowest of the low. Opposite to the static mountain peaks, the highest of the high. A system of balanced exchanges. The roar of impermanence versus changelessness, a unity of opposites. The waterfall perseveres, sleepless, always there, a universal renewal, yet the shape remains the same, not the same, but the same. A dense cohesiveness, almost ferocious, a phenomenon of the stream, a dangerous suction of gravitation pulling me, help, dragging my reluctant mind to a realization that change is real.

At the falls lookout, no tourists, some time alone together. A flash of color flits past me. We are not alone. A butterfly lands on Winky's back. A black butterfly with white dots in the middle of each wing and red dots inside sepia concentric circles. Like a target. The butterfly's sticky feet cling to Winky's shirt. I look closer at the butterfly waving its feelers. Ominous. Evil. I step back. The butterfly swivels in my direction. I move further away. What if. Butterflies bite. We fall silent and the ever present water falling roars. Winky shakes himself. Violently. And a man, where does he come from, gives the butterfly a silent command, the butterfly releases its grip on Winky and flies over to the man and lands on his hand. The man leans on the railing and nudges the butterfly to dance from his thumb to his forefinger and then back again, repeating the motion over and over the butterfly loops across his hand like a miniature circus performer. We leave the man and the butterfly in the hope they will establish a lasting friendship at least. We have that.

god forgive me for what
I am about to do

Notes

Uruguay. Walk into a country. Pumpinks in syrup. Buen suspiros artisanias. It's legal to buy 10 grams of weed. The guy on the ferry looking at his reflection in the window. Bobbing up and down in his seat the consequence of a diet of bread meat cheese sugar alcohol.

Eight am we are early, no rush, but queues begin forming at the terminal for the ferry to Colonia Del Sacramento, the old smuggling port of Uruguay.

Bliss ponders the word Terminal and its Terrible Meaning incurable lethal mortal deadly, a dead end, but not ours traveling somewhere possible for the sun shines today congratulating ourselves for arriving at the Terminal on time.

An old man sitting on the opposite side of the waiting room stares at me for twenty minutes. Longer and his grey whiskers, dark eyes unsmiling, has he a violet scarf, right, hat-less, cuffs, brown lace-ups, this unmoving figure gazes. Has he sat on a patch of superglue? Will it come away in sticky strands when he rises? Keeps laser watching directly at me and I pocket the stares, count the stares now mine for keeps, what have I done, but be anxious for what form takes a stare maybe arrows too easy could be whips or slinkies say shooting from his eyeballs. The air dances with this list oh my mind again give me sleep and the man stares at what am I. Stop looking at me. Question could I be that fascinating. No. Has he fallen asleep with his eyes open?

The dock, the ferry returns, nothing but chugging across the water to us at the Terminal here comes the ferry, bang on time.

Hop off the ferry in Colonia and experience the thrill of strolling into a country under a clear sky and sunshine as if popping out for a carton of milk. Inhale the scent of freshly mown lawns. Wednesday must be lawn mowing day in Colonia where gum trees remind us of home.

These modes of transport available in Colonia, bikes, scooters, golf carts, Thrifty car rental. Winky keen to rent a golf buggy. *No.* Too dangerous with Winky at the wheel, we will head for the other side of Uruguay and he'll keep going until we reach Brazil and how safe are those golf thingummies being at the mercy of South American drivers ranging from erratic to insane.

Barrio historica, the historic quarter ahhh perfection, the seventeenth century reaching for us without plans but to immerse ourselves in picturesque, charming, pristine, no crowds, no tour groups and relax in this air heavy with colorful decay absorbing calm how the sun shines through the leaves of trees creating dappled light also shadows of trunks make patterns of bark on the roughly hewn stones of old and on Portuguese style cottages, single story beauties a made-in-heaven village popped up from a perfect sea and remains preserved in this corner of Uruguay. Blink.

A cobbled stone lane and above our heads hangs a butterscotch glass street lantern illuminating the blue and white street sign, Calle de los Suspiros. *Sigh*. Street Of Sighs. Listen for the sighs as we step careful of uneven stones and sudden crevices easy to twist an ankle, we wobble wish for a walking stick, hold Winky's arm for support, all the way to another invasion of color continues to happen same as breathing.

Pink bougainvillea like ballerinas' pirouetting from the side of a stucco wall shading an old orange Vauxhall, its number plate 'LAA.' Well la la la clash of colors persuade me to think otherwise for orange meets pink love at first sight, a clashing leads to complexity, not such a bad thing, except for over-stimulation, Winky comes to a steep hill and recites 'the little red engine.' I think I can I think I can. Embrace chaos. Over there and here. This color war.

And everywhere vintage cars, retired cars, 'Cachilas' parked in laneways and on the sides of roads. Some preserved, others rusting, geranium plants and green ferns spilling from missing windows. Find a violet Volkswagen beside the buttery wall of this store, Tambor, instrumentos, artes, artesanias, mas. Music! Violet and yellow! Secondary colors in the tradition of complementary colors opposite each other on the color wheel blah blah in 1666 Sir Isaac Newton developed the first circular color diagram defining a harmonic visual experience and sense of order, speak of equilibrium opposing extreme unity leading to under-stimulation. We All live On A Yellow Submarine bash the bass drum and dance the conga line Aye Aye sir live a life of ease, of skies seas lah de dah Yellow Brick Road. This boy's too young to be singing the blues. Our future lies beyond the yellow brick road, it'll take a couple of vodka and tonics to get us to our feet again, for we believe we are violet and yellow dreaming the perfect match.

Follow an old woman walking with a stick, a sack on her back, she disappears into the sunshine or maybe a wash house, the maroon door falling from its hinges. Broken. Stranger things.

Over the drawbridge? Of course radiance upright of a white lighthouse, not too tall, among spruce trees, this beacon so crisp against the cloudless existing within its own realm of time, of polishing lamp, trimming the wick, as if never encountering storms or birds dashing against its lamp, or sea spray blurring the windows. I swear it's the front page of a picture book or a novel, To The Lighthouse...

And in front of a cafe, the waitress arranges checkered deckchairs like cubist flags ready for lunchtime patrons. What can Pumpinks in syrup be and purchase ten grams of weed, it's legal.

My own sense, sensing a patchwork of brighter colors and pastel borders around pink render and crumbling grey stones. Think ice-cream and candy and how the cookie crumbles.

Mid-morning on the harborside, music blares from loud speakers, Los Shakers 'It's My Party' the outdoor restaurants, empty except for Winky and Bliss sitting at a wobbly table and drinking dreadful coffee. Always. *Don't.* Winky insists on sweetness, a sleepy waiter plonks a muffin on a plate. The muffin looks like a turd.

Oh the blueness sea view and us wearing baggy t-shirts and baseball caps cripes a perfectly matched couple strolling by, maybe our age, except much slimmer and well-groomed in their chinos, panama hats and navy blazers. Why are we not like this couple? Why are we so ramshackle? Well please recall, opposites define a harmonic visual experience and a sense of order. But for the clothes.

And then the sight of three young backpackers sprawling on the pavement. They lean against their packs and sun themselves under a sign, 'Restaurant Lola' large letters painted with a flourish on the wall of a yacht club.

What's wrong with sitting on the ground? Winky and Bliss yes cool and hip, but once down on the ground, we can't get up, our knees creak as we kneel and struggle to rise above it. Above what. Aging. Yep that. It's a sign.

We know.

Avoid the souvenir shops. Limp towards the church, back to where we started, The Street of Sighs. Sighing hungry now.

A wine shop advertises tastings and lunch. Buen Suspiro, *artesanias gastronomica's dulces quesos vinos.* We choose a rickety table inside a stone room in a garden lined with spindly tables, all empty. Winky ducks his head. In the center of the stone wall hangs an oil painting of an English country garden glowing against the wall more than it is, this magical gem inside our cave of dim light and I think this hovel might once have been an old garden shed. Or a tomb.

Another extensive menu. Biblical. Dishes of locally sourced food, *part of the proposed Good Sigh. Share magical moments with your partner...* Chopped must mean sliced. Chopped Small Sigh, Chopped Sigh Flower, Chopped Big Sigh, South Sigh and Chopped Sighs of Nun.

Thinking of a meat cleaver.

The waiter brings us a platter of cheeses arranged according to shape. A row of eight triangles beside three columns of cubes beside twelve flat spheres of cheddar. Enough for ten people. Gasp. The waiter appears again with two more platters of cured meats, more cheese and some hot delicacies I don't remember.

Jesus. They're going to have to winch us outta here.

We finish the meal with pears poached in mint turning the pears Granny Smith green. Rich hey. We can't stand up.

Time moves with immeasurable slowness. The fault of the cheese. Of thinking, of sketching on a square of paper all there is makes this a moment of being drawn into the past permanent. And a desire to steal this Barrio Historico. Wishing. Maybe dismantle the entire village lit by a fierce but friendly sky and reconstruct it inside a portable Perspex box and keep it with me always.

five balls of butter

Notes

Five balls of butter for breakfast. Man with a tattooed arm wrapped in cling wrap. PV restaurante lounge.

Montevideo. Catch a bus from Colonia. Expect, you know, an ordinary bus. But. The plush seats a surprise. Nice. Then panic. God what if it's a tour bus. Is he a guide. Scrabbling in my bag for earplugs. It's okay. He's the ticket collector. Anyway, take precautions. Stuff the earplugs into my ears. What? What are you saying. I can't hear you.

First impressions as the bus arrives in Montevideo, a corroding city, strangely dark, a menacing darkness. I can hardly see. Nightmare world. A malevolent city. The avarice and self-centered mood of a colonial city. Oh right. The tinted bus windows are darkening the place. Darkly.

An hour's bumpy taxi ride to the hotel. Paranoia, again the lack of safety belts troubles my nerves and the cabbie listening to Highway To Hell.

The Radisson on Plaza Indepencia, a grubby hotel with an understaffed disinterested reception. Poor Winky spends ages of ages checking in. And he misses seeing the woman striding into the hotel lobby. Dazzling glaring blimey. Over six feet tall, tottering on thousand inch high heels covered in glitter. And her short dress covered in sequins. Her eyes weighed down with false eyelashes flapping to the center of heavily rouged cheeks. Her ballooning lips caked with crimson lip gloss and platinum hair swept high and cinched in a ponytail. A vision or a nightmare? An 'I Dream Of Jeannie' lookalike hooker? A transvestite? A showgirl? An iconic sex goddess? Woman not real, inhuman, her humanness buried within a parody of womankind. This creature. An exaggerated manifestation of femaleness. Never a baby or a child or a teenager, but a toddler balancing on stilettoes. Its chubby flesh awash with glitter. How much time does it take to assemble this outfit, this blinding persona? The enormity of the task. Her physical transformation into a visual spectacle. A gross theatrical spirit version of Barbarella. A beefy hyperbolic Barbie doll. *This splendor of woman as an extreme statement.*

Winky juggles forms and passports and breakfast vouchers. Hang on almost there.

Winky you'll never believe...

He turns away from the concierge's desk, just as the Queen of the Galaxy disappears leaving wisps of silver, an ephemeral trail across the lobby.

The night rain falls on a decadent ripeness. On the tawdry of Montevideo.

The cool climate forces me to wear all my summer clothes. A skirt over leggings, two or three t-shirts, socks with sandals, the look peculiar being surrounded by locals wearing thick winter garments, boots, fur-lined hooded jackets as if about to arrive in the South Pole. Do South Americans fear cold weather. Isn't it spring? I just don't get it. And they are staring at me.

In the restaurant recommended by the hotel bell hop, we encounter a plethora of wait staff. Restlessness. Heavy furniture. Zero diners as ten pm, the proper time for an evening meal. The drinks waiter hovers forever. Water sir. More wine sir. Yes and yes and yes. The waitress reappears between every mouthful of mediocre pasta. How is everything. Wisks the plates away. We are. Still chewing swallowing grasping after the food. Indigestion. Desert? We pay for our meal. Winky in shock at the bill. Ten dollars for the use of knives and forks. Wave of a spoon.

Outside rain on the litter on the streets on the shuttered shops shall we go. Giggling into the dark glare. Into the soulless emptiness.

The hotel breakfast enjoys spectacular views and an appetizing buffet. I watch a portly gentleman scoff five butter balls. First he concentrates for a whole minute on each butter ball arranged in a circle on his saucer. He begins a seduction of the greasy spheres, sliding the butterballs one by one between his pouting lips. Plump lips. Imagine a tiny voice crying, goodbye sweet world before disappearing down his throat. This sucking of butter balls arouses and repulses me go figure, the opposing, the rousing and the sickening feeling all at the same time. Puts me off my powdered eggs. Forever.

Ugly at another table, the sight of a man's tattooed arm bound in cling wrap. A rough guy all leathery and chains and the suffocating tattoo, eggs on toast for breakfast he should wear proper sleeves to hide the seeping and festering. Why wrap a tatt? Well. Apart from the fact that a new tattoo proves 'an exciting experience' for enthusiasts, a fresh tattoo is in reality, a vulnerable wound needing protection. Like the soul. So wrapping a tattoo in plastic prevents germs from infecting the open wound but doesn't allow the tattoo to breathe. Think smothered wound. A breeding ground for unpleasant bacteria. He must have worn cling wrap all night. Take it off. Ugh.

The PV Restaurente Lounge, a library cafe on Sarandi. Walk up an old marble staircase to an airy room lit by leadlight skylights and tall windows. Nibble scones, sip coffee, browse books. A fixed meal 'menu ejecutivo.' This comment by a Uruguayan. *Interesting restauration of an old house from 1900 or before. The library is beautiful and you can get very good advises from the helpers. The place inside has rooms where courses can be taken as writing, chorus or drawing. And the coffee place has a reduced proposal to eat and drink. Anyways, it is a very nice place to know.* Yes a very nice place to know. And free cutlery. Finally.

Return ferry from Montevideo to Buenos Aires and the luck of three seats to ourselves towards the front. In the smoke and muggy and dampness crowds of rollicking passengers shout at each other mighty such energized conversation shrillness this noise as if everyone aboard anticipates something extraordinary, as if these people have never left Uruguay, as if they have never been anywhere. Not even a bullfight.

A young guy bobs up from the seat in front of me. He is. Thin. He has a. Tan and he has. Sharp brown eyes darting from side to side looking around the ferry. A searching expression becomes animated, breaks into a manic grin. An excited person as if anticipating. He sinks back into his seat and turns to face the window fogged from sea spray and mist. He jiggles his head from side to side at his own reflection, makes admiring oohs and ahhs with his lips. Oops! He pops up again, half standing, looking over the seat, his excitement mounting, he trembles and smiles broadly at the other passengers, he sits down again and looks at his reflection in the window and practices various expressions and seems delighted with his appearance. The process continues for the entire trip. I want to hit him with a sledge hammer.

The ferry docks in Buenos Aires and everyone surges for the exit. As if trapped on the ark for months. Well. Taxis might be scarce at this hour.

The young guy leaps up and adjusts his backpack. His exhilaration makes him appear airborne. Before he steps onto the gangplank. Before he proceeds with whatever adventures. He hesitates and bows his head. He prays and holds up his right hand and makes the sign of the cross. Signum cruces, two fingers press together, a brief connection, heaven the forehead, lower, chest the earth and both shoulders, power and place and finally a light kiss on the thumb. Covering everything possible. Go forth young man. He bounds down the gangplank and disappears into the throng, into sin city. *God forgive me for what I am about to do...*

Cars Castro Che Cobblestones Cha Cha Cha

Notes

Cuba Havana. Holocaust. Hemingway. Victor Hugo. Man selling peanut brittle in the park. A pond in the shoe store. Floridito. Beer with tomato juice. Beer with lemon juice salt and ice. Bucanero beer. Cigarettes sixty cents for a packet of twenty. Early evening group of young kids girl spit on the ground. Safe to hitchhike. Fifty hitchhikers on the Auto Pista. Skippy and Flipper on television. The Giron museum. Best coffee at the crocodile park in Cuba. 'Coffee has a mysterious trade with the soul,' Jose Marti. Floridita Trinidad. The starving dog at San Francisco de Paula church on the Plaza Carillo. Maracas and fine china. Two men carrying a stuffed calf. Museo 1514 Quinze Catorze restaurant in Trinidad, masses of china and glassware. El Alba in Santa Clara, traditional plates cooked over an open fire. Film crew making a documentary. Chef pops out from the kitchen and dances while a waiter sings a shirt solo. Two women dancing in a liquor shop. The buzzards circling Cuba. Grass growing on the bus stop roof. Lobster live music La Cuenta Che cars Castro cobblestones cha cha cha. Close call in… and I pray to every god in the universe. Save me.

Midnight. A couple of soft-bellied capitalists, land in aha Cuba, a time-warp idyll lies in the deep waters of vintage cars, Castro, Che, cobblestones, cha cha cha. This bark-less island, where dogs do not bark. Listen. No barking. An island without rough seas. An island devoid of advertising. An island prolific with abundant vegetation, wild amaranth, singing birds, swamps, straits, springs, streams, gulfs, tidal flats, high mountains and ten deep rivers.

Jose Marti International Airport, named after Jose Marti the Cuban poet, messianic figure and revolutionary activist. What's in a name.

Two blonde girls with 'don't-mess-with-us' expressions race just ahead of their taut figures wearing denim shorts weaving their way through the immigration queue. Intense eyes dart from tourist to tourist. The girls mutter into walkie-talkies. No drama. Walk away. What are they searching for.

The bare and beige and mammoth. Arrivals hall. Staff floating in brown uniforms. Nothing to do. But constant suspicion levitating in groups of two and three chatting to each other. Officials sporting military badges wander about. Doing nothing. Nothing doing. We wait for our luggage. Two hours. A million belt rotations. The baggage carousel spits out single bags at random. I picture the baggage handler sorting through the contents of each suitcase before allowing it to go through. Thumbing my books. Delighted hands ruffling my underwear, socks. Why bother to fold. Anything. Her or he or both no hurry we have all night, I imagine this like everything we're here in the real Havana our bloodshot eyes waiting for two suitcases oh yes and every piece of luggage must be x-rayed for. Contraband? Of some sort I guess and I can't imagine what in my ignorance of smugglers. So we wait. Surly guards lead sniffer dogs. Diligent beagles sniff backpacks, satchels, haversacks, rolling totes and suitcases. Those dogs seem happy and much busier than all of us, the guards, the airport staff without job descriptions, the weary passengers, the browns the beige the officials. Winky and me on Cuban soil.

One o'clock in the morning. Exit the airport through automatic doors to find a huge crowd of Cubans lingering outside leading into. Half the population of Havana. Here. These peopling people their sole purpose to stare at the tourists and travelers coming out of the arrivals hall and we arrive again to a soundless barrage shoulder to shoulder men and women. Hundreds of hard eyes. Imprisoned eyes watching the bedraggled tourists. Hard of hard eyes. Bars on eyes prevented from leaving this island prison. A million eyes maybe waiting for Jose Marti to appear, to preach, *man loves liberty, even if he does not know it. He is driven by it and flees from where it does not exist.* A billion lost eyes look beyond, not dreaming but yearning, wishing, for what they really crave. Escape. To swim across the gulf stream to Florida. Find the life most Cubans desire, La Vida En Rosa - life in the pink.

Ancient jalopies vintage cars the beauty everywhere in a country not allowed to buy, sell or trade new vehicles. The flash of headlights, brings life to these beasts. Yank tanks revving or idling Pontiacs, Cadillacs, Plymouths, Buicks, Chevrolets, Dodges, Fords, Chryslers. For the love of cars. Fifty thousand old gas-guzzlers. Piles of rust balancing on four tires. Some more loved, immaculately preserved, the chrome tailfins polished until gleaming. And every car a national treasure, no matter what condition. These cherished heirlooms roam the byways and highways of Cuba. Enterprising Cubans develop outstanding ingenuity as do-it-yourself mechanics combining sap and mineral spirits, concocting brake fluid by mixing oil, shampoo and soap. Replacing V8 engines with Fiat four-cylinders. Cannibalizing Russian Ladas and Volga's for parts. Extracting differentials from old Land Rovers. Installing propane gas tanks in the trunks. Stuffing guavas and bananas up leaky radiators. Recycling old trucks of no use anymore and building submarines out of the carcasses and escaping to Florida. This I do not know. Here in the dark where engines of wrecks, bangers, heaps, rattletraps belch fumes as they pull in and out of car spaces.

Silvio our driver, sent from the B&B to meet us. His eyes warmer and shinier than the old white Jaguar he points to. My heart. The tattered leather seat of the Jag. The wooden dashboard. Beautiful. A pine tree shaped air freshener hangs from the rear view mirror. A purring black Buick pulls up. The driver waves to Silvio. They wind windows down and stop for a brief chat. For in Havana, everyone knows everyone.

Silvio crunches the gears and lurches onto the dimly lit streets. In the outskirts of Havana, groups of men play cards or dice at tables set up on the curb under a street light. This absence of televisions or computers. But sometimes a square blue light from a living room.

Unable to afford cars, inadequate public transport, Cubans share rides, walk the miles, yet going nowhere in these empty streets. 'A Song of the Road.' *The people walk with zeal, But wheresoe'r the highways tend, Be sure there's nothing at the end.* Idea of wandering without purpose. Open the door to the dark. Of the unknown. The blank eyes, the deep sadness. Where to go where they come from, this searching for self, failing to find a way out.

La Rosa D'Ortega the casa particulare (bed and breakfast) situated in La Vibora, once an exclusive neighborhood filled with estates, mansions and grand houses now in a state of neglect and disrepair.

The day beaten by oppressive heat. And a billboard of Fidel and brother Raul smiling compassionately and crying Libertad Ya!!! At Cubans trying to survive on twenty dollars a month. Revolution years stir the days. The difficult legacy. The leaders old, many dying. Fidel remains, his beard growing longer and longer from a face unchanged.

Silvio drives us into the old city, a relic of sunlight and mystery and passion and politics and the saddest beauty. Pain evaporates. This whirlwind time in a free-falling life. A world crumbling from the inside out. Dilapidated buildings, abandoned gardens, rusting wrought iron. I trip on the rough cobblestones and avoid the many potholes and whine about my knees. Winky walks backwards to stay in step with me.

Naivety ignites a lack of guerrilla enthusiasm. Be inconspicuous.

Hidden shops stock unrefrigerated meat secreted inside dark rooms glimpsed through a single open door.

Who says all revolutions rot? Somewhere on this island exists a department of security with steel doors leading to a labyrinth of hallways and armed guards interrogating political prisoners inside cold brightly lit rooms and people's lives hinge on the generosity of the Revolution. The time of truth, the time when a poet might beg, *tell truth tell truth let anything happen let them rip the beloved pages.*

La Habana, a novelist's riff. Tricks of the tongue taken apart and transfigured by Guillermo Cabrera Infante, *Havana the name of a city which is just a beautyfoul corruption of Savanna/ Sabannah/ Sabana/ Abanna/ Havannah/ Havana/*

Habana/ La Habana/ Avana in Italics Cyrillically Gabana, and the Spanish panner.

And think Havana, Historia, Holocaust, Hugo, Hemingway. We cannot escape the bearded fishin' shootin' drinkin' American writer. The famous-for-daiquiris Bar El Floridita where Hemmingway drank. Beer with tomato juice. Beer with lemon juice salt and ice. And in one corner of Bar El Floridita sits a brass bust of Papa Hemmingway has an eerie resemblance to bearded Winky.

La Habana Vieja, the few gentrified streets, the narrow lanes of the old town. Cubans crouch in doorways or gutters or balance on rickety stools. One woman perches on a stack of egg cartons. At the sight of Winky, she cries,

Ernest Hemingwaaaay!

Dinosaur Hemmingway. Remember his disparaging comments about race, 'chinks' 'niggers' 'kikes' 'rummies' and women, 'bitches,' 'victimizers,' 'ruiners of men,' *she's not a bad girl, she's friendly and she's all right.'* His obsession with man against the forces of nature, acceptable in *that* time, I suppose. Ernest Hemmingway wrestling the sea, storm, fish. Hemmingway sucking the country dry of alcohol. Every bar in Cuba proclaims Hemmingway drank there. Winky and Bliss follow in his footsteps. Chin chin, salud, cheers big ears, bottoms up, may we have no regrets, lift a glass to my mouth, look at you and sigh.

On the shore at Cojimar, we find another bust of Papa Hemmingway. What no cocktail? Or maybe too many makes him greenish. Eyebrows knowingly raised. His forehead wrinkling into a grin like Top Cat. And an epitaph carved in stone, *here's to looking like movie stars, hard-boiled writing like writer stars, partying like rock stars and fucking like porn stars...for the sun also rises...*

The month of May in old Havana. On a splendid day some offers of, be a spy, marry me, buy my turtle and on the harbor, groups of Cubans dance in heavy rain. Kiss each other with delight. Take photos of others frolicking. This celebration as if rainfall falls for the first time. A woman sitting near us explains that rain on the first of May means very good luck.

A man appears dressed in a white suit. He clutches his balls, and with his other hand holds up his trousers so as not to get the hem of his pants wet as he carefully steps across an overflowing drain

A chubby black girl sits on a low wall in a park. Her plump legs swing as she leans forward. Her hair parted down the middle, tied into cute pigtails with rosy ribbons matching her dress. She lowers her head, gazing at the puddle in front of her. A skinny white boy strides up and jumps in the puddle. He twirls, prances, turns and faces the girl. Her stoic expression expects the inevitable. The boy kicks water directly at her. She frowns. Demon boy takes running leaps, skidding, still kicking, making waves and a whoosh of water saturates the girl. She holds fast and does not move. No words express. She sticks out her bottom lip. Nasty boy becomes frenetic, kicking more and more water at the poor girl. His face unseen. But I imagine it twisting with evil pleasure.

Continue walking, desperate for coffee. The coffee in Havana proves unpleasant and milky. Who cares about coffee? Well of course, it keeps us going like the sap and spirits fueling those antique cars. Winky says, you choose a place. But if it is a frightful place. Well then he complains, my fault. Steer him into a shabby café with plastic chairs at a redwood table on uneven brick paving in an enclosed courtyard. Order two coffees. Americano with cream. The waiter looks surprised, but does not question us. The weak coffee tastes ominous. Paper lanterns swing in a non-existent breeze here in the stillness of this mind-sapping heat. I take shelter in the shade of a covered walkway near an arcade. Fan myself with a map of Havana. Inside the cafe, eight Asian men eat noodles from bowls held close to their open mouths. This café is a Chinese restaurant. This dilapidated place, all Bliss's fault unable to read the signs. Oh god. Coffee in a Chinese restaurant in Cuba. What could be better.

Havana authentic and gritty does not live in the present, but inside its own present of our past oh the internet now available in the lobbies of five star hotels and mobile phones sell, but for the waiting.

The Havana of endless chitchat and flojos. Everywhere this stance of dark figures framed in doorways. Tall muscular black men, one hand on their hip and an arm leaning on the architraves facing the street and behind them, unlit rooms and roofs sinking into shadows and maybe on one wall hangs an indecipherable lithography, a sanctified stamp.

Look a pond filled with stagnant water in the window of a footwear store. Can't think of a reason to put a pond in a shoe shop.

Now insane light skims Havana's sun setting. A city place where nobody knows what might happen next. What to believe. Experience life within the infinite value of a particular moment. Bongo drums banging from the seafront. Such pleasures not planned or captured by photographic images.

Years of upheaval weigh the people down. The people possess a dream-like quality. Inner reserves filled with strength, pride and a love of life. This intricacy and ambiguity. Those rhythmic beats of hip swiveling musica Cubana cha cha cha's from every open doorway. Music dances along pavements always riddled with huge potholes. Children blow soap bubbles.

Girls cuddle rag dolls. Shirtless boys throw baseballs in the dusty barefoot streets. An old man sells peanut brittle to the patrons of an outdoor cafe. We find an art installation of steel fish suspended in metal cages glinting in the late afternoon sun.

Groups of Cuban teenagers crowd the sidewalks of Plaza De La Revolucion. The anger and frustration of a hard-faced girl spitting on the ground. What else to do. In this city of fish art dancing in the rain air loud with the sound of guitars from heaven and viva el 1st de Mayo and Hemingway writing, *Brother, don't let anybody tell you there isn't plenty of water between Havana and Key West.*

Well follow the days in Havana, still be still this suffering heat.

We stagger across a moat into the Castillo de la Real Fuerza set back from the mouth of the harbor. Stone walls keep out the heat. Rest for a while on a deep stone windowsill. Gaze at the harbor. Think dreamy thoughts, picking violets in the snow, turning slowly like a carousal and underwater reeds in a river, swimming in the sea, opening the refrigerator door, yes retrieve ice-cubes place on my forehead, a slight breeze now stay here. Do you comprehend no. Listen to. Winky climbing the stairs of the watchtower.

When I get to the top level of the tower, come outside and take a picture of me.

Okay.

And I imagine the watchtower to be thousands of meters high.

The man loves his photo taken on or in front of valley views, canyons, mountains, waterfalls, statues and at the top historical monuments, pagodas, buildings, towers, bridges, cathedrals, temples, whoa honey please, don't go so close to the edge, come back to the car, that lake is frozen.

Close my eyes for a minute. Hear a quiet cough. Open my eyes. A security guard stands in front of me. Worry. Maybe it's forbidden to sit on the window sill. She holds out her open hand. In her palm lie several coins. She smiles with enthusiasm. A torrent of Spanish. I shake my head. She beams with acknowledgment.

You from?

Australia.

Change yes? You have change in Australia?

Confusion. Wondering why she wants to know about Australian currency. Smile. Oh yes we have coins, but not one and two cent coins. We have five, ten, twenty and fifty cent pieces.

Now her confusion wondering what the fuck I'm talking about. But she proceeds, enticingly fingering the coins in her hand.

Cuc cuc. Peso convertibles. Gambio gambio.

The money appears to be Euros and some other coins. Does she want more money? Is she asking for a bribe?

The guard becomes more excited. She points to the coins. She speaks in a louder voice,

Gambio. Gambio.

Bliss recognizes that word.

Err. No we don't have Gambios in Australia. We have banks.

She frowns. She becomes more and more insistent.

Cuc cuc cuc.

I should know what the word means. Nope. Does she want me to somehow identify each coin? I peer at the coins.

I'm sorry but I don't know.

Ease myself off the window ledge. Try to sidle away. Winky appears purple and furious.

I've been waiting and waiting up that goddamn tower. What are you doing?

Explain about the coins. How I don't understand why the guard wants me to describe Australian money and our banking system. She explains in Spanish. They both laugh apologetically. Winky gives her some pesos and she hands him her whole coin collection.

Lots of tourists give her tips in Euros and other currency. She can't use them here. She was hoping you could exchange her money for the equivalent value in pesos.

Oh is that why she kept saying cuc cuc?

Yes. Cuc is the local currency.

Heading for the exit, I notice the tower. A modest tower, only three levels. Poor Winky waiting all that time for me to come outside and take a photograph of him waving on the top of the inadequate tower with its whopping brass bell, *all along the watchtower...*

Our Jaguar taxi speeds through the suburbs of Havana to Romeo y Julieta, a cigar factory in Pina del Rio. On the way we pass places we are not supposed to see, the boulevards during pre-revolution times once opulent regal colonnades, now gaunt and starved and haunted by the lingering stench of colonialism and corruption. The streets as if edged with suffering buildings. This lost grandeur of Havana sticks in my mind like a shock of *anything can happen.*

From a rooftop bar (Hemingway drank here) the heat of the noonday sun heightens the colors of terracotta rooftops and blonde stucco buildings with aqua shutters in the whole of Havana.

We hire Romario, a youngish driver and his cuenta propista to drive us to Trinidad. He guarantees his taxi to be a Toyota Camry equipped with seat belts. The cost for three days, there and back, works out the same price as renting a car. Romario is beyond excited at the prospect of driving us to Trinidad. He arrives accompanied by a pretty black girl wearing a colorful cotton blouse, shorts and a flower in her hair dressed up for a holiday. She sniffs copiously while holding a wad of serviettes. Romario explains the situation.

Os present a mi nyovia Zamira. Va a cumplir manana esta muy resfriada. No podia dejaria en casa todo el fin de semana.

Winky translates.

Romario's girlfriend Zamira has a shocking cold. It's her birthday tomorrow. He couldn't leave her home alone all weekend.

Okay.

We turn onto the bumpy Autopista Nacional. Grass grows among the potholes on this national freeway. Hundreds of hopeful hitchhikers wave pesos at the few passing vehicles. An occasional rusting truck clatters past us. Romario drives as carefully as possible. Romario plans big things for our trip.

Primero vamos a visitor el parquet de crocodrilos.

The crocodile park and wildlife sanctuary and apparently very popular but I hate crocodiles, killing machines, basking in the sunshine. The park keeper ties a baby croc's jaws together with rope and convinces a reluctant Winky to drape it around his neck. I take a photograph of their ghastly grins.

Beside a stream, the park cafe serves hot strong coffee, the best in Cuba. A blessing! For coffee *illuminates the inner depths and sends them as warm and beautiful concepts to the mouth.* These warm and beautiful concepts light up my sleepy brain. One last sip of the warm and beautiful concepts. Here in this sanctuary for murderous creatures and strong coffee.

Next stop. Playa Giron. Romario drives us past an Australian sugar mill near Playa Largo where Fidel Castro ordered the mobilization of troops and from there, he led the battle operations. Romario, born into revolution, fervently explains the battles and Castro's excellent reforms in Cuba. Romario hell-bent on converting us to communism and we nod, of course, no worries. You must understand the importance of *becoming* the place.

The Museo Giron, a museum (a shed) documenting the CIA-backed invasion by Cuban exiles of Playa Largo and Playa Giron. Outside the museum, a British Sea Fury aircraft and a battle fatigued tank nestle in a garden bed of wilting flowers. The tank, a greenish color with the turret cemented to a jutting pipe. The gun doesn't look real. Where are the windows. How do the soldiers find where they are going? I'm not even going to answer that question. Has the sun fried your brain? Don't you realize it's not a real tank? Sad, worn out plane. A fake canon. Remnants from an exhausted war resting in collapsing foliage.

We view an exhibition of black and white photographs with slightly inflammatory text below each picture, detailing the events of the invasion.

The deep changes process gave the lands to the ones who works it and discards the latifundium system forever. Latifundium? *The economic/social laws dictated by the revolutionary government enlarged more and more the abyss between the reaction and the town. A hard blow to Yankee imperialism and its domestic flunkees...Before the UN, the imperialism presented a blatant tall story to conceal their guilt in the attack to Cuban airports. The artful mercenary bombing of April 15th caused the popular repulse... That is what they can't forgive us. That we are there in their noses and that we have made a socialist revolution in the own noses of The United States. Swear to defend until the last drop of blood this revolution of the humble ones, by the humble ones and for the humble ones. They defeated mercenaries eluded responsibilities.*

They all came as cooks! Their testimonies were similar, they all came deceived. Others simply were just cooks or their missions were purely spiritual.

Mercenaries in the noses of The United States. Tall stories, popular repulse and the idea of disguising domestic flunkies and cooks as mercenaries. Have they misspelled cook and mean, crooks?

Crocodiles, stray dogs and scattered vultures circling high in the sky. The only creatures in Cuba. And these buzzards possess American mafia spirits that once used crime to control the island. Banished criminals waiting for another chance.

We stop at a roadside restaurant, this shady outdoor structure, flower-patterned plastic covers the tables, a well-stocked bar in one corner (waiting no doubt for Hemmingway). We invite Romario and Zamira to join us. They reluctantly sit down. The waitress, note pad at the ready, glances with disapproving eyes at Romario and Zamira. *Hoy no hay langostinos.* No lobster today. The warm water lobster caught from the Caribbean sea by artisanal fishermen from June to January. The lost expression on Romario's face. This combination of hatred and misery. For unknown to us, lobster is never served to the locals. Lobster is reserved exclusively for tourists. Forbidden lobster. And the waitress seems afraid. Without the proper papers, the possession of lobster, beef and shrimp results in long-term imprisonment.

Global comparisons. In Cuba, cigarettes cost sixty cents for a packet of twenty. Australian cigarettes, twenty-five dollars, the second most expensive in the world and a lobster can cost eighty dollars and upwards and in Australia, it isn't safe to hitchhike, anywhere.

Trinidad of emaciated horses pulling homemade carts along cobblestone lanes. This ancient colonial town, once rich from a past of sugar cane and slaves. Now the slave owner's villa, transformed into Museo Romantico. Bars secure every window and door. Not that romantic.

A woman crouches on the front steps of her narrow house, part of a row, the facades painted in canary, ginger, magenta. She wears a cherry dress and on her head, an orange turban. The woman's skin is pure black. Her limbs the width of a twig, making her a figure of connecting lines against intense colors. And the whites of her eyes flash starvation from a different era.

Harsh sunshine persuades the colors of Trinidad to be cleaner and blinding. Stroll down Calle Jesus Maria. Glance in the window of a tiny house. The interior of overwhelming red and nosy me staring into a living room awash with red sofas, red rugs, red table cloth, red curtains, red roses and towering over the room, a red crucifix. Walk away quickly. Escape the intensity of this blast of meaty red. As if this house maybe some sort of animal with an exposed beating heart and blood soaked organs and him saying don't worry.

A couple of three level concrete apartment blocks outside the old town. Soviet-era architecture springing up from the hard ground. A stark contrast to the colonial buildings and rows of richly painted cottages crowding the historical center. These cinder blocks, each level painted in candy colors like cake frosting or sherbet or pastel toilet paper. The kind of colors chosen by girly girls, gentle rose, sugary green and lilac at the top. A confectionery low-rise of mismatched pastel cubes. In contrast, the red window shutters like gashes held together with white steel bars. This vibrant down-at-heel toy land against the dazzling sky. A load of washing hangs over the side of a balcony. The clothes in order of size and color. Four pairs of jeans, three pairs of naive shorts, pockets turned inside out and a child's faded gingham dress.

We turn back towards the old town. The dusty roads, no life, except for a horse drawn cart, the driver's shirt a daub of navy seems static against iridescent green walls. His thin, half-starved horse, rib cage visible, drags its legs clip clop the only sound. And always siesta time, no shade anywhere, the ruthless sun scolding Winky and Bliss, our presence discordant with the landscape, we do not belong here, perspiring in the heat, the silence, the sickly colors, as obvious as a dull politician at a flamboyant transvestite's funeral. Lean on Winky. Keep walking. Along more streets crowded with rundown cottages. People loll in doorways. Nothing to do. Leisure predominant. The occasional group of old men playing checkers. Paint peeling from the walls. These watered down colors of leftover brilliance from the old town. A truck like a cage on wheels rumbles past. The hood camouflaged spruce and tan. Cafeteria Viscaya across the lane. On the front cartoon letters illustrating images of a hopeful hamburger with melting cheese like a pillow stuffed between the bread. Beside the burger an unappetizing yellow milkshake and a pizza resembling a pool of vomit, the white lines representing steam give the pizza an air of surprise. What is happening. On another wall, someone has scrawled three lines of script. CDR Con Fidel y Raul Defendemos la Revolucion. And a faded version, faint words of something important but not anymore, now scrubbed away and painted over with a stronger more emphatic statement. *Defendemos la Revolucion...*

On a corner, sits a squat bungalow with a terracotta roof and open window framing the sign, *El Frutijugo*. Strings of garlic, gourds and unripe plantains hang above mini pineapples, an *Agricultura Urbana,* harvesting fruit far too soon and a TV aerial, angrily bent out of shape.

A wire mannequin stands just inside the entrance of our hotel lobby. This headless, armless and topless Thing draped in a ballooning white satin skirt with a matching ruffle ruching the copious amount of cloth. A fluffy and frivolous dress with nylon roses surrounding the waist. And beside this creature someone propped a wire parasol in what appears to be a bulimic attitude. From underneath the skirt runs an electrical cord plugged into a power point. This dummy lamp.

Over on Calle General Lino Perez, we discover a second Floridita (Hemingway also drank here). Gasp. Air conditioning. Glad of an escape from the midday heat. The modern bar graced with the presence of a bloated Irishman gulping a tumbler of Scotch. He hears our accent and slurs,

Australian eh? Yer a ways from home...

Three musicians strike up a salsa beat. Half a heart. But the money. The tip. The Irishman now resting his head on the table. A waiter saunters over. He frowns at the drunk. *In God We Trust,* embroidered on the pocket his trousers.

Inside a wine shop, the two storekeepers, both middle-aged women, sell booze and sing the heart and soul of Cuba. Their hips gyrate under matching uniforms of light brown skirts and shirts, identical pearl brooches pinned to brown striped scarves. The women spin around the store. They thrust out a leg here and there and hop behind the counter and ring up a purchase. All the time singing, *Aye yi yi yi otro timbalero, ay candela candela candela me quem a Mama Aaaay.* Meaning, the mouse went crazy. Dance for fun. I burn well. Something like that, the heart and soul and wine.

The Plaza Carillo. In the water-starved garden of San Francisco de Paula church. This hairless puppy curled up under a dead shrub. A mauve greyish dog, almost indistinguishable, its color blending with the gravel and dry leaves. Is it alive. Ghost dog half-starved in that starving garden. Does anything thrive here? Yes. Color.

The owner sits on the front step of his restaurant. His tiny moustache and careful Spanish curls combed just so. More a shop than restaurant. Every surface of every table laden with bone china, antique silverware, crystal glasses, lace napkins, fresh roses and fine white linen cloths speaks to me a hoarder by nature. Yet candle light. Romance. Raise a sparkle glass, feel the weight of it, the shine of it and wonder about all these spoils of the revolution looted from an underground hiding place.

We dine heartlessly on lobster.

Dancers wave maracas and rumba to the beat of African drums, fine old porcelain rattling sing Cuban folk songs as the headwaiter sings a rousing duet with the chef, while two men carry a stuffed calf, taxidermy specimen lying on what appears to be a stretcher. Sneak out of the kitchen and tiptoe past the musicians.

Over there, the raucous table of a New Zealand film crew here to make a documentary about dogs and their owners in Cuba. One of the crew, a snooty female appears swaying before us. Her waist-length curly hair makes her withered and lined face seem a hundred years old. Her attitude, I'm a film director therefore a much more interesting person than both of you and I'm only talking to you because I am drunk. It transpires the film crew hit a snag in Havana when they discovered Cuban dog owners don't speak English. Winky and Bliss feeling smug at such stupidity expecting the world to speak English. The director gives us an airy wave and gushes. Keep an eye out for The Hounds of Havana.

Inside we are howling.

An English couple start chatting to us. Wayne and Jane *somewhat* dowdy and tipsy. Just arrived in Trinidad two hours ago.

We dropped our knapsacks at the casa particular what a dump and came straight here and now we can't remember the address of the casa.

Winky doesn't have enough cash to pay for our meal and Wayne roars,

I'll give you money. I have tons of it.

Embarrassed Winky borrows forty dollars. Insists on Wayne and Jane coming back to our hotel so we can repay the money. Two o'clock in the morning after a stiff whiskey, Wayne and Jane pass out on the sofa in the hotel lobby. Winky and the concierge bundle Wayne and a bleary-eyed Jane into a waiting cab whisking them away into the dark streets of Trinidad. And we never see them again.

Sunday. Light rainfall. Steamy day. Romario drives us up into the Escambray mountains where Che and Castro plotted the revolution. From a lookout, view the ocean and Trinidad far below.

The thick leaves of prickly pear cacti are carved with love hearts, smiley faces, signatures, *Carlos Omar Belen was here 2013. Harriet loves Gerald XOXO. Diego and Charlotte.* Autographs disfiguring cacti unprotected from the pain inflicted by what? A car key? A pen knife? At what point in time does it occur to someone to carve initials onto the inoffensive leaves of a succulent plant? Vain tourists needing to write their names on every part of the natural world. Gaze at the landscape, rich emerald against a dull sky. Think of humans touching the sky and initialing the clouds with a black felt-tipped pen.

Down the mountainside. Our taxi, the only car on this curved road, its gravel surface slippery from the rain. Going about thirty kilometers an hour. On a sharp bend, Romario loses control of his taxi, slides off the road and tips sideways and as if in slow motion, flings me over to Winky's side of the back seat. The car careens sideways on two wheels. Romario turns the steering wheel as far left as possible as the side of the car slams into a row of cement bollards beside the gravel. Don't remember any noises. Brakes screeching and metal scraping. Nobody screams. None of us make a sound. Feel as if I am in a bubble rolling over and over and thinking, is this it, praying, *help us,* to the god I don't believe in. Somehow a distraught Romario manages to get all four wheels back on the asphalt. He pulls up on the opposite side of the road. Zamira in shock, blows her nose and stares straight ahead. Romario begins to cry and says in broken English,

Lo siento mucho I am so so sorry.

Winky and Bliss reach across from the back seat and pat him on the shoulder.

We're fine. Everybody's ok. Don't worry about it.

And we leap out of the car. Romario starts sobbing again at the sight of the damage to his precious vehicle. The paint-work badly scratched and the side trim and hubcaps gone missing. Winky walks over to the spot where the car hurtled off the road and knocked over two bollards. He searches the surrounding bushes nearest to the bollards and finds one of the missing parts. On the other side of the bollards, Winky sees a twenty-meter drop. My spirit hovers over a hill over-looking farmland. In the distance, hello a farmer maneuvers his tractor through the fields, do you know what. No cars on the road. No other transportation in sight. No one to rescue us if. Nothing but misty rain to sooth us. But the moment invincible make it through saved by a bollard and I stare dreamily at the countryside as I touch my uninjured self and soul two words circulating my consciousness, I might write a hundred times on every cloud in the sky, *thank you thank you thank you* at that time and forever after, a grateful spirit recites the same mantra, *thank you thank you thank you.* And we. Continue on our journey. A braver Bliss. Amazed at how unruffled I feel. Not at all disturbed or frightened by our near death experience. But a shaken Winky keeps repeating under his breath,

We would have disappeared into that horrible jungle never ever to be found. Gone. Forever. Gone. Straight over the side. Buried by dense foliage. Swallowed by a tropical forest.

Ssshhh. Everything is fine. Stop freaking out.

Last stop. Sunday in Santa Clara. Church bells ring in the square. Grass grows on the bus stop roof. Santa Clara, a shrine to the rebel Che fighting and winning the historic battle against Battista. A proud Romario proclaims,

The last of the Cuban revolution, forcing Battista to flee the country and allowing Fidel to gain power.

Romario convincing us of the virtues of socialism. He points out the train tracks where the battle took place, a short walk from Parque Vidal. He drives us through crowded slums and rows of Soviet style concrete housing to visit the Museo Historica De La Revolucion and Mausoleo Che Guevara, a mile from the center of town. Visible from every direction, the bronze statue of Che in military fatigues and holding a rifle.

On the way to the mausoleum, we pass three or four men killing a pig on the side of the laneway. Lunch. One man raises a gigantic dagger. Beside the men, a heap of smoking coals. I cover my eyes. Too much of a coward to witness bloodshed before meeting Che.

The Museo Historica De La Revolucion and Mausoleo. Exhibits of Che's water bottle, his gun, medical certificates, photographs of Che as a wild haired handsome man smoking a Cuban cigar and playing golf. Simple worn out theatrics masking a desperate war.

Underground. Walk through to the dim mausoleum illuminated by an eternal flame. Can't stop thinking about the murder and dismembering of the pig in the street. Why turn away? From the pig murder. Steel myself. And look. Experience the horror. Here stands the eternal coward viewing the burial site of sixteen guerrilla fighters and the iconic Che. Am I brave for not wanting to witness an animal dying in the dirt. Tell me.

Romario drives us to the town center. Look back at the statue of Che, surrounded by a parade ground fit for Stalin himself. Is the statue incompatible with the dusty laneways, shantytown shacks and local pig killers? Or is it me that is wrong?

Leaving Cuba today hours waiting in the forever in the airport check-in in the queuing watch staff examine every passport, this search for fake identities.

A bald man in front of me. Too close. Blerg. An arc of short black hair rims his ears as if the hair on his head has left his head and taken up residence around his ears. Move away from the ears hear behind us, a British couple complaining to each other about Havana.

Rotten food and the whole place so filthy.

Winky and I shrug. Go home. Some people deserve to be exiles. Visualize the venom dripping from Hemingway's pen at the British couple's lack of vision. Hemmingway writes, *The Limeys don't try hard enough, Limeys give up.* Then they are executed.

Bridge Of Sighs

Notes

Lima. Small excitable men. Afternoon tea, cocktail country, dirt/ sand hills beside the beach, don't go near the edge, oh alright, go near the edge if you fall over I'm going to leave you there. A hand emerges from the ticket booth and the many dolls at the Archbishop's Palace. The band plays on. Man walking down street carrying an old fashioned sewing machine. Plastic figurine of Spiderman on the shelf at the Gambio. Soccer bar on Plaza San Martin, giant corn and the man with a pudding bowl haircut cut straight round his head like a monk. Lunch at Estadio. Bridge of Sighs. Chocolate bread. Painted Statue of a Saint Bernard dog wearing a back pack, makeup and sitting in a park . Taxi drivers ask policemen for directions. The hotel receptionist gives us a warm chocolate chip cookie. Scintillating.

Two nights in hazy Lima's silvery light reflecting a patina of grime. Not a pretty city, home of the Spanish Inquisition plundering South America. In the distance, shantytowns crawl across hills. Risk a kidnapping take a taxi, the congested road, on one side the cold waters of the Pacific and on the left a soaring vertical cliff face and the road runs through it, dividing mountain and sea, rich and poor.

What if Lima takes a human form. Imagine a volatile, intense person worrying about exposing its dirty laundry, a heavy smoker, an exotic cocktail of corruption, mysterious, perplexing as in civilized. But not civilized. A resentful city stripped of its Inca gold. Lima presses heavy what do I do, in this strangest saddest city in the whole world with its solemn brass bands, Moorish carved balconies and small excitable men.

We walk in the park. The park on the edge of a cliff. Hang back with my vertigo fear, don't go near the, Winky goes right to the, no thoughts of safety, the cliff without fencing, what if you trip or stumble or the rocks crumble under your feet, my thoughts but him lacking resistance, sprints this urgency to the, straightaway, shall I go in the opposite direction always this disgruntle, oh alright then, go near the edge, do I care. And if you fall off, I'm going to leave you down there, no one to rescue you in this other time zone of hungry seas, well you know I won't and I can't speak the language, you need to grow wings for the life you lead.

The hotel serves cups of tea from perfect pyramid shapes. Three dimensional tea bags attached with the paper shape of a tiny green leaf. The tea bag handle. I steal one.

What about that guy lighting a cigarette, look at his pudding bowl haircut, straight hair running full circle around his head like Friar Tuck. Or a skirt. Light a candle to whoever gave you that atrocious cut, oh but the skirt swings in time with an old sewing machine he carries, rusting its weight, does it work, the friar's found object and he hisses steam and blood looks like a stormy night.

Winky changes some money in a grubby hole-in-the-wall Gambio. On a high shelf behind the counter stands a plastic figurine of Spiderman. How are you here. Why. Sign the paper hand over the money. You look plastic in your tight outfit scaling a Church bells ringing and shaking you off.

In the center of town, crowded streets, buses, the milling, the closeness full of revolution, a horn sounding banshee impatience too many bumping into walls, twisted faces, stumpy bodies shouldering past us. Winky shouts,

Not a pretty race of people are they?

Ssshh. *Quiet.* They might carry knives.

Plaza San Martin. We eat lunch at Estadio, a noisy soccer bar full of cheering men, chocolate bread and corn kernels the size of marbles.

In a park, sits a painted statue of a Saint Bernard dog with a lavender backpack. The dog appears to be wearing eye make-up and lipstick. Are you leaving Lima.

If a taxi driver gets lost, he stops and asks a policeman for directions.

We never find the Bridge of Sighs.

Sigh.

Black Jesus Me Salvation

Notes

Panama. On every flight, as the plane lands, the passengers break out into spontaneous applause. Four rosary beads hail Mary crucifixes and Nazarene de Portebelo hanging from rear view mirror. Tables in restaurants, either low or too high. Coughing in a restaurant. A giant knife fork and spoon stuck on the outside wall of a restaurant. Black pelicans. Number plate: Jesus me salvation. Stylish cookies. Shopping mall, HR hair revolution, spray on hair. Shop called Tactical Army. Lot of chit chat, nose picking, standing in doorways with one hand on the hip. Panama canal tight fit for the ships. Las Clementinas cafe and bar, obnoxious American twentysomethings. Cab driver imitating Skippy.

We place our precious lives in the control of those who transport us. A short flight from Lima to Panama. Winky hoping for a glimpse of the famous canal before our plane lands. Read to distract myself from where I am in a plane landing always read for the take off and the. This book, The Skeptical Romancer selected travel writings by W. Somerset Maugham engrosses me, engross being an ugly word, think of another, captivating no absorbing yes the idea of gross is what is gross is this engrossing no but the book, now an extra limb, an extension of my fingers and therefore I am. Calm. Ignore the surroundings. Not worrying about anything. At peace. Read the same paragraph three times. Concentrate. Calmer than calm. Winky pats me on the thigh. Winky's pale face.

That's his second attempt.

What?

The pilot can't seem to land the plane. He's going round now for the third time.

Every fiber, muscle and sinew in my body tenses. My heart starts pounding.

Whaaaat! Are you serious? Why are you telling me this? Do you think the pilot is a trainee? A learner? Don't tell me. Oh my god.

For the first time, I notice fear in Winky's eyes.

It's going to be a rough landing. He's coming in too high and too fast.

We hold each other. I love you. I love you too. My palms sweat, whimper. Repeat my mantra to every god in the universe, *get us on the ground get us on the ground get us on the ground get us on the ground.* Hear the thump of the wheels dropping.

He's too high. And, Christ he's too fast. Oh well third time lucky.

Then screeching and a terrific thump. The plane touches down and streaks along the runway. The pilot brakes so hard. Every organ in my body flips over and changes places. Swear my hair defies gravity and stands straight up from my scalp.

No one makes a sound, except a toddler shrieking, *Chocola-tina Chocolatina.* The plane halts. The passengers cheer loudly and break out into spontaneous applause. Winky and I look at each other.

Thank God thank God thank God.

We have landed.

The hotel fails to produce transport from the airport as promised and with fingers crossed, we flag a taxi. Winky enjoys practicing his Spanish with cabbies. For God's sake, don't talk to the cab drivers. South Americans prefer to talk face to face. Taxis driven by compact dark men happy to converse. Who gesture emphatically while speeding along freeways. Neither hand on the steering wheel. Turning to face us, yabber yabber, ignoring the road ahead. Freaks me out.

The taxi's number plate, Jesus Me Salvation. Strands of rosary beads and Hail Mary crucifixes hang from the rear view mirror. Beside these medallions, the picture of a black Jesus with wide crazed eyes and white lather cascading from his lips and over his beard. Nazareno de Portobelo, a statue of the Black Christ that washed up in a crate onto the beach of San Pedro de La Escucha and when opened, the deadly plague devastating the population at the time, vanishes. Miraculous. Traffic zips by. I need a miracle. My face white with fright staring at the Black Christ swinging over the dashboard and wondering why be scared. The Black Christ watches over us. But why does the Black Christ foam at the mouth? Ernesto the cab driver, turns around to face us and grins,

Where you from?

He accelerates. My jaw tenses and I make a fist and it's not from rage well a moderate amount of rage and not being able to relax, silent begging, *pleeeease watch the road.* Winky leans forward,

We're Australian.

I jab Winky in the leg.

Don't encourage him.

Ernesto's eyes sparkle with delight. A quick look at the cars in front, he changes lanes so fast throwing me against Winky. Then swivels his head around chortling his best imitation of an Australian accent.

Gaddaymite.

He takes both hands off the wheel oh my god he makes paw motions and bobs up and down, imitating Skippy, the bush kangaroo hopping, for God's Sake watch the road. Ernesto flips back to driving mode. I mean these few seconds feel like you know imminent death, me with my head in my hands, not smiling, how is this possible. Jesus Me Salvation. Save me Jesus.

Panama. High-rise steel and glass, a vast and modern city on the heels of election fever, the new president or benevolent dictator promising to fix supermarket prices of rice, beans, powdered milk, beef, eggs, yucca, cheese and bread and remove mosquito breeding sites declared a Dengue fever zone hazy on the epidemic details for a city is a city is a city and this city is the same as most.

At the four-star hotel, Winky complains about the absent driver. The concierge hands me a brown paper bag containing two warm chocolate chip cookies and offers a suite and the breakfast buffet at no extra cost plus Wolfgang the hotel manager will chauffer us around the old town and drop us at his favorite restaurant. All of which somehow terrifies me, except the cookies.

Las Clementinas, an intimate bar and café subtle with potted palms and classic Panamanian dishes basking in an art deco glow. Order sweet plantains with melted Brie topped with spicy raspadura sauce followed by a Caribbean seafood stew.

We sit close to the bar. Too close. Two young American couples perch on barstools, their knees almost touch our ears. American of perfect blow-dried hair, manicures, pressed jeans, dry cleaned silk shirts, four pimple-less humans, sparkle lips drink glasses of white wine. Vow never to look in a mirror again. Vow to iron my clothes. Vow to become thin. Vow to be young. None of this will ever happen ha so eavesdrop their baffling conversation as they examine maps and tourist brochures of Panama.

Yeah oh and oh you know ooh stop it!

Our taxi cost us $3.50.

Henry's mum said stay within these streets.

Uh so cool.

Vanessa literally told us the stores that sell stolen goods.

How do we find them?

Oh Gosh yeah yeah that's what I was going to do!

Are you sure this is ahh up-to-date?

Yeah. Do you guys wanna go to....?

I wanna.. Oops... Right.

I wanna go there. Oh. Ok.

What happened?

They said it doesn't rain at night here.

Really! Darn it.

Panama Canal. Well it's a tight fit for the ships. We reach the observation deck on the fourth floor. From there observe the locks emptying. The locks open, close and refill, it seems so unnecessary Winky bounces around with excitement, wanting to visit the Panama Canal, since the age of ten.

In the museum, a life-size captain's deck with control panel complete with levers, switches, handsets, lights, dials and a variety of buttons. The chance to be the boss of the Panama Canal. Winky steers a simulated ship through the lock transit via a curving 3D movie screen. When I take the helm. The film speeds up. Watch what happens wow people, trucks cars zipping to and fro like frantic ants and matchbox toys on either side of the canal. Fill my ship with navy and banana containers stacked like toy blocks. A boat races past me. Squirts water from its backside. Shoots through the lock gates. Catch up to the boat. Stop and wait for water to drain and the gates to open. Tugboats puffing wisps of smoke, rush here and there. A tug at my side directs me to the second canal or back to the first canal. Where is the Atlantic Sea? Not sure. Maybe ahead. Concentration lapses. Lose my boat in the canal. Somewhere sinking. That sinking feeling. I am. A hopeless ship's captain.

A strip mall, the size of a small island. Mundane shops for the masses. Stores selling Stylish Cookies. HR hair revolution spray (multiple colors to choose from). Fashion shops named Gloss, Very Sexy, Dark Stage, Moose and Whoops. Winky disappears into Tactical Army. Winky mesmerized by automatic weapons, guns, pistols, hunting knives and surveillance gear. *Men.*

Sightseeing makes me stupid. Makes me think ridiculous things. This time, the gigantic fork and spoon glued to a building. These utensils as big as oak trees. Maybe a restaurant for giants, a bistro with supersized food. I do not want to go there and anyway it's closed.

The hotel porter carries our bags to the elevator. Winky goes ahead to book transport to the airport. With obvious fascination, the porter stares at me and murmurs,

Your beautiful green blue eyes.

Ruins

Notes

Peru. Cake, wheel barrows full of corn, sugarcane and cooked meat are popular. Mother in the ladies restroom allowing her child to play with the toilet plunger. Have to put paper in bin, not the toilet. The sign, No bote los papeles al inodoro.

Machu Picchu. Café, mountain view, jungle, passion fruit vine, leaves moving, What tourists wear when traveling. Train from Machu Picchu. Guy in a lime wig waving candy, in a rainbow satin outfit, in a wolf mask.

Cusco. Peppers stuffed with quinoa, with creamy goat's cheese and honey. Prawns coated with quinoa and deep fried. Passionfruit and basil. Altitude sickness. Pisco with tumbo, mint, chili and ginger. Tumbo? Inca tour of rocks. The steps. Incas' painting of The Last Supper. Home-made blue corn juice. Tour guide shouting.

Cusco. The airport, a shit fight. Twenty minutes searching for our tour guide, Chimichui Adventures. Already an adventure.

Not fun. There, the half-hearted wave of a placard. The guide in his thirties, casual, well-dressed and intelligent looking like a university professor, which he probably is. Where were you? The guide smiles,

Oh yes nowhere. Here all the time! But too tired to hold up my sign at the arrivals gate.

A cardboard sign.

Put my fingers in my ears, I can't hear you, la la la, listen. No. Cusco balances on a high plateau on the brink of the Andes at over ten thousand feet carrying the nights and days high. Don't tell me.

Wait in the hotel lobby for a room. Help myself to several cups of coca tea. The Indians call it Cuca, cocaine leaves torn from a plant of significant medicinal virtues. Sway, heal me, tonight orange moon, and gentiles, wizards and diviners offer Cuca to the idols, which ones, all of them, Cuca leaves, more valuable to the Incas than gold, silver or precious stones. Pick the leaves by hand and dry them in the sun for dampness injures the leaves the leaves the leaves.

The guide explains our itinerary. I stop listening. More swaying my head floating away from my body, energy what energy drains from my body, can't. Stand up, intense shakes, I am unable. In the drugging somehow. Is it the tea? More tea? The guide warns us about altitude sickness. Huh? What's altitude sickness? I struggle to get up from the sofa. My body sliding into oblivion, the weight of my feet, my arms am I heavy as lead what do I do. Do the Incas scalp their victims? Stop grinning Rip Van Winkle there is no goddamn air it's rough being numb and weak. The guide advises.

You need to lie down for a few hours.

The hotel gives us a choice of two rooms. Really don't care blerg. Need more. Air. Take the biggest room. There must be. Stagger into a pleasant, fall onto the bed. The concierge beams.

We'll turn on the oxygen.

Where is the oxygen? Don't we have any?

Groggy. Babble. Winky thinks I'm over reacting. Am not. I am dying. Slowly.

Sleep in the extra oxygen for a few hours. Walk down a cobblestone street leading to Plaza des Armas, the main square. In this altitude, the low oxygen levels, many tourists slump on benches and stare into space. My legs turn to mush. Chest tightening. My eyes water. Wheeze. Walk slower even totter slow motion drag me. I am. The slowest person in the universe. Barely move. Fairy steps. Twinkle toes. Winky walks backwards to keep up with me. Again.

Oh boo hoo. How come you haven't got altitude sickness?

I have plenty of red blood cells.

And I don't, where have my blood cells. Gone. Do I own any, the delirium searching for red blood cells, are they red, I suppose so. I am. Still dying.

Tomorrow the fortress Sacsayhuaman, translates as 'speckled head.' And do you know Cusco in Quechua means navel. Cute don't you think? Nup. Beyond caring about speckles, blood cells or navels. The non-air is killing me. I am. Almost dead.

Our hotel recommends a local restaurant. Winky orders peppers stuffed with creamy goat's cheese and honey, deep fried prawns with passionfruit and basil. I have. No appetite. I have. Shriveling taste buds. Feeling like the atmosphere clubbing me to death. Order a tumbo with mint, chili and ginger. Divine. Don't feel so bad now. Tumbo. A pisco sour. Eighty percent alcohol. I am. Coming back to life. Where are we. Sliding too.

The Inca ruin. Enormous polygonal rocks arranged in a large field. With nowhere to sit. The rocks, no me, the struggle to stand up, to keep standing. For eternity. Can I sit on the ground. The guide explains how the Incas used natural fiber ropes to haul these diorite blocks a distance of fifteen kilometers and after placing them on limestone foundations, the rocks were hewn with stone hammers and bronze chisels. Exhausting. And a hundred milling tour groups. I can't. The rocks look like giant grey corn kernels. And the high stone walls, a monumental scale of impenetrable. Beautiful. And a desperate wish. If only. There were a couple of smaller boulders. To sit on. In this field. I am. About to fall to the ground. In the power of. The altitude horror witch casting her, no thinning the air, give me some, no, she takes it all, sucks on it. Suck it up. The guide announces,

Next, we go up there.

A thousand steps. Oh hell. Millions of steps. Drag my sandbag legs. Moan. Think again. I am going to. Die.

This is about. Altitude sickness on the internet, read ghoulish stories about tourists dying from altitude sickness, first suffering from nausea, coughing up blood, slipping into a coma and death. Da da. Happens in *minutes*. Nobody knows why. Sternly hold up my thumb and forefinger indicating a space of a few millimeters. This close to death. I could feel my brain swelling. A contrite Winky suggests.

Why don't you have a nice hot shower?

The hotel bathroom. I stare uncomprehendingly at the seven taps in the shower cubicle. Turn one tap on. A blinding jet of hot water hits me in the eyes. Examine the instructions etched into a tin plate screwed to the marble tiles. How to operate Peruvian faucets. Ur.

The shower has three knobs and four watering can where the water get out.

1 hot. 2 cold. 3 this one control the exit if water by the watering can or by the spout of the bathtub according to the small part of knobs handle 3.

Position A: the water comes by the spout of the bathtub.

Position B: the water comes by the watering can of the roof.

Position C: the water comes by the watering can of the wall.

What will happen if I turn them all on at once? Well I could drown. Death. Again.

The poor sewage systems in South America mean that used toilet paper cannot be flushed. The sign in every loo: *No bote los papeles al inodoro.* Please place in the bin. And I always remember just after I flush.

The Inca version of The Last Supper. Subtle Peruvian aspects indicate rebellious attitudes towards the Spanish. Christ and his Caucasian disciples eat roast guinea pig, Andean cheese and hot peppers. They drink purple chicha (corn juice). Betrayer of the Incas, the conquistador Pizzaro, is portrayed as a dark skinned Judas. Llamas replace horses. Is the painting a masterpiece. No. And roast guinea pig oh god in heaven.

We are.

On our way to Ollantaytambo! Beautiful this name, whisper Ollantaytambo. Oll an tay tam bo. Like a poem of pearl words,

oll
an
tay
tam
bo

Of thoughts but for the bumps and holes in the untarred road and a maniac bus driver driving the tour bus. Maybe it's worth this trouble and terror just to say Oll an tay tam bo. The bus whips around hairpin turns. We hurtle a thousand meters down the mountain. Disclaimers? Well they are non-existent in Peru.

And the lower we go, the more normal I feel. Really goes. Peace in my guts. Is this. A dream. Energy lost returns, the prodigal me. Steady. Stay cool. Don't get too excited. Scream. As normal as I am able to feel. Altitude sickness evaporates.

As the bus zooms through The Sacred Valley. Our guide shouts,

Sheep sheep. Cows cows. Looky. Looky.

We know these animals and they are not that interesting. But here. *Beneath* broken mountain ranges and plunging canyons in the valley of the Urubumba, women lay washing out to dry on the grass.

The recommended clothing for Peru. *Garments that layer, short sleeved shirts, slacks, sweaters, a warm fuzzy jacket, a hat, a scarf. Shorts are not recommended (read the article on 'Bugs that Bite') Strong footwear is critical. If planning to hike the Inca trail come prepared with your regular mountaineering gear.* We do not possess any mountaineering gear. A practical Winky purchases walking sticks in Cusco.

Again, I wear all my clothes. At once and perfect the look of an escapee from some institution thank god for sunglasses.

The heart-stopping Inca trail as crowded as Times Square on a Saturday night and they say plenty of tourists become irrational from exhaustion and fall over the side. Oh well. We are. Too weary for the Inca Trail and catch the bus to Machu Picchu. A twenty-minute trip each way. This compact Mercedes Benz bus races up a slippery dirt road cut into sheer granite, clinging to the side of precipices. Winky, Bliss and thirty silent tourists grip the seat in front. A pile of rubble half covers the road. Oh yes an avalanche last month forcing the government to close Machu Picchu could happen again any-time and. A loss of tourist dollars. The bus driver accelerates a hundred miles, a hundred miles, the time to meditate, to transcend this life, on the threshold of hysteria. More hairpin turns. Don't look out the window. The steep drop of dizzying. Pinnacles, dense jungle, tropical forests. Lovely. Our hands weep the euphoria of certain death. Death, my old friend. My mind chants, the higher you go, the further the. Reluctance in this hallucinogenic spiraling scene of mists and majestic mountains. Tell myself, surreal fecundity proves too grandiose for a brain as bare as mine. This scene is Not Real. It is theatre. A huge canvas backdrop of sublime green landscape. The bus lurching and my heart lurches martyrdom with each decel-eration, each turn and the jolts of slamming brakes. God in heaven. Anything possible in these resplendent heights for a cowardly pilgrim. Remember when the explorers wielding ma-chetes, hack through the undergrowth. How these explorers might scorn my trepidation. Winky and Bliss in this careening bus and the explorers riding heavily laden mules. All of us in danger of rolling down the treacherous pathways and precipi-tous slopes, hundreds of feet into the Urubamba River raging below. All of us searching for The Lost City of The Incas.

And my fear casts out the frustrating years of youth fluffing about, roaming in ignorance from country to country. Fear relives those times, gives the years a different perspective. Because right now, right at this moment, because of this actual moment in time and still shaking from the bus journey, we arrive in Machu Picchu fear leading me down stone steps, leads me round a large rock and there lies stupendous. The canyon.

A magical city. An Inca edifice. Incomparable. Lamas inhabiting the rock terraces and funerary caves and stone dwellings, this sacred shrine its existence buried for centuries. Windows frame the clear sky, grass and watchful mountains. Squares. Raving now. Is Machu Picchu a fortress or a royal garden or a religious place of contemplation? Nobody knows. No written records exist. The meaning and reason for Machu Picchu disappearing with the people of the sun, bathing newborn babies in icy water to toughen the child for a life of cold and hardship.

The mythical site, once lost, now found and lost again in the trampling of tourists, two thousand trespassers per day, the numbers increasing daily, thousands desecrating the magic, threatening the delicate balance of nature. You must. Tread carefully.

Right.

Winky decides to climb 2693 feet up Montana Waynapiccu.

Meet me in the cafe in two hours.

The last bus leaves at five. If you miss it you'll have to hike down that mountain.

Which is worse, the descent or those lunatic Peruvian bus drivers.

I am. Alone. On Machu Picchu unable to locate the exit lost in the lost city and thinking on a ledge for an hour and wishing to carve a piece of Machu Picchu and store it in my heart. But that's. Desecration.

In the cafe near the entrance, I wait perching on a stool at a table, the jungle lurking below and hear rustling in the dense vines and think snakes cougars cannibals. The branches and leaves move vigorously and I pull my feet away from. A striped sleeve emerges from the leaves and a small hand reaches for a piece of fruit growing from the vine. The child's face hidden, just the hand reaching out.

Two hours and Winky nowhere to be seen.

A tour group of battery-driven grey nomads congregates at the turnstiles. One really old man wears a t-shirt that says 'old guys rule.' Lame and not true. People, when traveling, tend to wear outfits they would never consider wearing at home. Woven hats, iridescent leggings with shorts, socks with sandals, shirts with stupid slogans Take A Hike, Hola Amigos, What Happens in the Camper Stays in the Camper.

Still no Winky.

What happens. In the.

At ten minutes to five, Winky appears drenched in perspiration.

Did you reach the top?

He nods, unable to speak.

I thought you were dead.

His wordless eyes glaze and every vein on his face turns dark purple.

You're one of those people. Aren't you.

And I gesture at the geriatric tour group.

We begin. The descent to Ollantaytambo.

And gaining what treasures from this steep journey. Nothing, I think. And everything. Not stamina. I am I am I am. Minus an inner core. What I am, a woman made of butter right here a glut of fear careening down and the rear of the bus slipping sideways in the mud on every bend. Of the avalanche in my mind. Whoa. Exhale. Claim to drift through the world. Fly across oceans. Relentless and ruthless journeys, faith in strangers, away the familiar goes, thrown off balance. Nothing and everything belongs to me all the real things, fog to breath air, impulsive dreams impulse, the sky continues above waiting for me and longing for a slug of nerve dulling whiskey.

5

Teapot Land

Notes

New Zealand. Pram museum, drive in radishes, teapot land, Invercargill, a basilica, the Robyn hood milk bar, Stu's fly shop. Leather walls, copper curtains. Fence made of old shoes. Sad-faced man carrying a ceramic elephant like a baby. Nasty child marching round the park. More angry boys. Woman saying, what they did to my son was just outrageous. On a calendar: may your life be like wildflower growing freely in the beauty and joy of each day! Front page of the press newspaper: Is a woman ever happy with her breasts? Black cows on the side of the steep hills. Sheep dying on the ledge of a volcano. The house, the floors, the pig. The pork doesn't arrive. The flies.

At midnight. Guzzling free wine, champagne from the lounge and more on the flight for three-hours, it's appropriate to enter New Zealand and be hammered, justifies the thought, well its *only* New Zealand, an island with a reputation for

weirdness. Remember the man in Dunedin whacking an innocent pedestrian with a live rabbit.

New Zealand, its effusive population greets strangers, hiya
hello how are you hi there hey hi. What the. This friendliness
takes everyone by surprise and the fact that.

Auckland means oak-land.

Somehow in Thames, an historic mining town not far
from Auckland's somewhere hot mud pools, acidic springs,
disgusting the idea of marinating in sludge, the sight of children and parents slathering themselves in a slurry of decomposing microorganisms. Who in their right mind. Winky's eyes
brighten.

But it's beneficial for the health.

Don't you dare, the mud is filthy and we don't have any
towels.

Somehow, come across this lone house, the flat roof
hidden from view. A cube. Tiny. Desolate. White. Neat. Square.
Bare. Stark. Full of nothing in the brightness of the day. An
ultramarine trim matching the blue front door. As if a white
block drops from heaven and extracts strips of sky on the way
down, landing in the center of a perfect lawn, minus garden
beds, trees, shrubs, just a row of ten plastic pots the two front
window ledges. These emerald, magenta, aqua, silver and gold
pots. A rainbow testament to individuality. But all the plants
dead. This conundrum, chooses and arranges plastic colors,
doesn't help, the flowers struggle to survive and lose the will
to live.

In the center of Thames stands a paper-mache donkey, old
hippy donkey wearing a checkered blanket tied with a tawny
cord, a paisley bandana supports pointy ears, a polka dot ker-
chief knotted around its neck from which hangs a crocheted
bag, for shopping. Heehaw. The donkey's soulful glass eyes stare

into the distance at nothing, drawing breath through enormous nostrils. All the better to smell us getting closer and closer.

The lingerie shop window, can you bear a panorama evoking a seedy but flimsy nineteen fifties horror flick. Saucy cartoons of a red bra and knickers with a black lace trim and dismembered dolls pinned to a chartreuse partition, the backdrop for three armless mannequins, two headless, one legless dressed in a body hugging orange slip. Another, its legs severed mid-thigh, wears black bikini pants and a camisole. The fifth just a torso plus a head and neck the width of its head and hot pink hair tied in a ponytail with a white bow. Perky dummies hacked to pieces. A nasty sordid display of lust set against squalid partitions. And large black type spans the length of the window. EROTIC DREAMZ. Below a sign claims, *Erotic Dreamz in the back half of the shop.* The sign on the door says closed. What happens are they. Self-combusting EROTIC DREAMZ, no burning EROTIC DRFEAMZ, no bad spelling, no, whip EROTIC DREAMS into submission. I can't think what. Goes on in the back of the shop.

A mystery café, grey weatherboard slats and white woodwork echo a genteel era. The remains of a counter, an inadequate number of tables and chairs. A blackboard hangs in the window. The blackboard shouts, *What's On!* Then a blank space, a black hole. There is. Nothing on in the mysterious. We cannot ignore the facts. Nothing happening here.

Wellington. Homemade crumpets for breakfast, indulge yourself, take morning walks, pretend to be normal, run-of-the-mill, all along the waterfront, a sad-faced man hurries past wearing a flannel shirt and stained overalls, ketchup I think. He cradles a large ceramic elephant in his hairy arms. Why so sad elephant man? Catches my mid-air stare, does curiosity motivate him, wondering what are you looking at nosy woman. He breaks into a run. Don't drop your elephant.

What's the rush, keep walking, over there, point enthusiastically at a wooden post. Someone transforms the post by outlining two bolts with a black marker creating real eyeballs and also drawn a nose around this metal plate and a smile with no teeth. Smile. People transform random objects with paint and felt-tipped pens all over the world. No one knows why. Winky smiles, unimpressed.

Pier Five for dinner. Rustic. Spacious. That warehouse atmosphere with beams and a beaming waiter sits us slap up against a colossal pillar. It looms. It's intrusive. I feel as if we are suddenly a threesome, Winky, me and the pillar.

Why does it upset you so much? Doesn't bother me.

I feel as if the bloody thing is leaning on me. At home, do we choose to sit against a wall or a veranda post or a supporting beam or whatever while we eat? Do we?

Winky remains unsympathetic.

Think of it as your new friend, like the smiley post on the wharf.

Arm in arm, stroll along the boardwalk, follow the night under a half moon, stars, soft breezes, a marquee, a roped entrance you must be a special to enter and from inside, the sound of a raging celebration. A wrap party for a movie shot recently in Wellington. The Hobbit or The Insatiable Moon or The Most Fun You Can Have Dying. That marquee pulsating with dancing revelers, their shadows overlap against the tent's canvas, as if a beast filled with lights and twisting shapes attacks the waterfront. This monster tent that ate Wellington rears up and invades Pier Five and devours that smug waiter who forces innocent couples to sit beside lurking pillars. The party marquee excluding the starry-eyed couple wishing to be in there, instead of on the outside getting old.

The National Museum of Te Papa's nickname the 'Papa' known as a scotch egg, slick and crumbly on the outside, but not much in the middle. And where are the dinosaurs? I discover a little skeleton under the escalator.

At least they saved one baby dinosaur.

Winky laughs.

Yeah right, that's a horse.

Winky obsesses,

Not one single Aboriginal left after the Maoris arrived in New Zealand and ate the lot of them.

A twenty minute ferry ride across choppy water to Days Bay. Winky and Bliss brave gusts of ocean air on the top deck. As the boat docks, I notice six fat women waiting on the wharf. The women wear rainbow tutus, frizzy wigs, fishnet tights, lace-up satin bodices exposing rolls of flesh. They titter like strange tropical birds and climb raucously aboard the ferry. I think that. The people seem like fun in Days Bay.

Find a warm café and order two mugs of chili hot chocolate.

Winky collects shells along the sandy bayside. Bliss rests on a park bench and waits for him. A plump boy in a fiery t-shirt marches around the park. The child shouts,

HUP HUP HUP

HUP HUP HUP HUP.

Non-stop, he circles families picnicking on the grass. He leers at smooching couples. Roars past groups queuing for coffee and cake at the kiosk. Heads turn. Everyone smiles. How cute. Such determination. This miniature monster, hands clasped together, chin pressing on his chest, face frowning with concentration, a furious fascist marshalling his fictitious army. That alarming sound spitting from his mouth,

HUP HUP HUP HUP HUP HUP HUP HUP HUP.

I want to grab him by the shoulders and scream *shut the fuck up*. But a dictator marches to his own self-made war and starts throwing stones at the seagulls. Hup hup hup you little shit.

Scan the shoreline. Winky in the distance, the size of a walnut. Winky enjoying the breezes. His pockets full of seashells.

In Days Bay, we pass a weatherboard bungalow, the exterior decorated with every imaginable seafaring object, all miniature. A nautical Disneyworld of tiny cannons, lighthouses, mermaids, life buoys. Anchors away. On the porch, the owner in a captain's hat. He tinkers with a model battleship. A retired admiral? Or a sailor deprived of toys as a child. Winky grins,

Ahoy!

We catch the Interislander ferry across Cook Strait to Picton in the south island, unbridling, hold your breath scenery, music mountains sing to the soul. And at the base of a mountain, sits the tiniest white hut. Snug and vulnerable, the shack glows like a jewel on a strip of sand against forbidding forests reaching for me. At least I imagine. So.

Wine country. Empty roads. Peace. Breathtaking the ice-topped ranges contemplating from high, the grape vines. Bliss behind the wheel of a rental car, alps framing acres and acres of grapevines the epiphany of astonishment. The hills are alive in Blenheim.

And driving across the south island wild grasses, some sheep in isolation, the bubbling brook gives way to a waterfall, this sense of victory, the open-mouthed divine and distant crags dazzling always this intake of breath, before reaching Greymouth.

Where we stay.

They call this line of sheds a 'resort.' Tinpot cabins strung across a hillside, miles from anywhere. A tall woman welcomes us. Her close-cropped grey hair, knitted polo neck sweater, tweed skirt like a schoolmistress casting a disapproving expression at Winky and Bliss booking into the honeymoon suite.

A brief lie down.

In the 'resort' bar, a lone man perches on a wine barrel and watches football on a television screen. Step into the dining room shall we, well the usual strangeness of eating in a restaurant without diners and thinking of barren lands and loud music and how oppressing this is and in the far corner a closed shutter for serving meals from the kitchen. We order two entrees and two mains now a blank for memories disappear in emptiness maybe seafood I guess a fish memory. Wait and wait. This slow death, morbid guzzling at least we have wine, forty-five minutes later, there is. A Deafening Crash. The shutter rolls up and an arm pushes a plate of food through to the counter. A male voice shouts something unintelligible. The screen slams shut. Weird. A dumb waiter. Wine on an empty stomach gazes at Winky eating his entree. After twenty minutes, the screen shoots up and the chef shoves another appetizer through followed by a screech. Winky mutters,

Christ. The kitchen must be short staffed.

The process continues for hours. The food delivery growing more and more erratic, accompanied by loud curses of dammit, shit, fuck a duck, fuck oh fuck. The school mistress rushes in and out of the kitchen. We hear the thumping sound of someone stumbling around the kitchen, of utensils and pots crashing to the floor.

I think that woman is beating up the chef.

I'll go and have a squizz at what's going on.

Winky returns after a short time.

The cook is blind drunk. As a skunk.

Hokitika. Speed along State Highway 6 and another immense uninhabited landscape. The occasional roadside 'bach'
the term for a weekender or a desolate farmhouse set back
in an overgrown meadow. And always no one in sight as if
every human attends a function we know nothing about or we
are the last remaining humans on earth but for the numerous
sheep. Not that we care. Peace expecting more peace our story
spans the sea and beyond the horizon

On a deserted beach, we find hundreds of grey, black,
white pebbles plus rocks stacked one on top of the other along-
side gnarled driftwood some hefty, some ancient vagrants,
some poor twigs tangle together as if dancing on twisted limbs.
The smallest rock piles, careful assemblages of stubborn hob-
bits facing the future. We shall not be moved. Monuments on
the sand. And these words written on a stone, BACK DOWN.
Other stones signed with love, K8 agreed to bungee Pip from
Norwich. Amber 2010 Essex xoxox. Kate & Nicole 2010 lovin
it xxx. Sticks poke up from between granite boulders, a thousand arms reaching to heaven. A white perpendicular stick not
bent like the others. Who makes these sculptures? Extra-ter-
restrial backpackers? The occult? A religious sect? Or do wild
waves wash up debris and voila enchanted stones. Easy.

Winky spreads both arms in a magnanimous gesture,

It's all supposed to mean, an individual visited this particular beach, they make their presence known. *I was here.*

Like a demented owl, I ask,

Who? *Who* was here? Who? And who cares?

Everybody from here.

The rearranging of natural surroundings by the hand of
man. What possesses a person to alter nature leave their mark

on this beach. What if all these individuals return at the same time. Relive the moment, the sands choking with humanity as each person stands proudly pointing at their creation and pronouncing,

I was here.

The air trumpets a secret in the absence of who was here and what remains, the *why* and the *why not* and that abundance, the irrefutable presence of their efforts. For the true meaning of 'I was here' results in signing pebbles with kisses, hugs, promises. Come back, promise me.

From Wanaka to Queenstown. Driving down a steep descent, round crazy sharp bends, brakes groaning, an extraordinary landscape forces us to pull the car over, gape at the view, the colors, the complexity, the vastness, the magnificence, the majesty and, until I remove my sunglasses, a surprising amount of pinkness.

A group of giants live behind quaint Queenstown. Wave to those Remarkables frowning at me from the Devils Staircase. Live up to your namesake. And they do. High on high. A remarkable presence guarding the township, the terrain, the blue blue lakes. Those Remarkables understand all the world around and inside. Me reading a poem (?) written on a stone wall beside Lake Wakatipu.

Balclutha to Glimmerburn
to Glendhu Bay.
Winter arrives on time
in a glitzblitz of powdery snow.

And under the blue blue sky, an inflamed midday sun, a steamboat steams across the *glitzblitz* Sunshine bay. The Remarkables scowl at bad-tempered seagulls too lazy to fly, pecking at flotsam, squawking over fish heads decomposing on the sand, where families picnic on mohair blankets and pour tea from tartan patterned thermoses. Ask the gulls, the debris, the lapping water, the tattooed backpackers biting into Man Killer Devil Burgers, the butchers working in the butchery and all the insular picnickers, What does it feel like to live in paradise?

Arrowtown. A Chinese gold digger's hut, yellowing newspaper pasted on its walls holding up rusting tin roofs, dot a hillside sharing the land with lime trees, white blossoms and looming in the background, purple peaks must be heaven.

And a winery not far from heaven. Winky negotiates the winding dirt one-way track clinging to the side of a cliff. On our left a soaring rock face and to the right a sheer drop. Close my eyes. Panic about oncoming traffic. Do many drivers, intoxicated after an hour of wine tasting, plunge into the ravine below.

At the end of the road, a swathe of tulips and orange lichen sticks to the base of trees outside the winery's tasting room. On a patch of gravel stands a sculpture of a female figure, constructed of driftwood and riding a twig bicycle. Her hair a violent conglomeration of sticks. Shudder at the sight of her skeletal frame so frightening, brings back evil childhood nightmares of figures made of branches wielding axes.

I'd like to set her on fire.

Burning woman.

Winky steers me towards the cellar door.

Don't you dare.

On the road to Fiordland, at a garden café, a blowsy waitress with protruding teeth and braided hair, storms over to us and whips out her notepad. She recommends the date scones. A year later we return for more scones.

Milford Sound, carved for one hundred thousand years by glaciers and according to Kipling, the eighth wonder of the world. Wait until he tastes the date scones.

At the boat terminal, massive iron blowflies decorate the walls. Hairy bugs freaks ugly sculptures, laying their eggs, shitting on ice-cream, crawling up my leg, attacking me, the philistine querying is that art no yes no. Winky leans close to my ear. Bzzzzzzz.

Shudders.

On the sightseeing cruise, enchanting Fiords lowering clouds from the sky by invisible strings, clouds drifting among giant rock faces reflecting that silvery sheen of deepest green water. Hopeful clouds speaking to the mountains, *we want to be part of you, we want to soften your cragginess, we want to comfort your leafy surfaces.* Clouds? Or mists? Or vapors? How could I not know?

And I run from one side of the deck to the other, experiencing the views through the lens of my camera, taking thousands of photos and seeing nothing. This blindness.

Of explorers wearing yellow life jackets in Kayaks, skim across the still water, stupendous rocks dwarfing these banana shapes paddling towards the cliffs hungry for kayakers swishing close to the rush of waterfalls and a mountain opens its cave-like mouth and swallows them whole.

The tour brochure says waterfalls multiply with magnificent effect during and after rain.

Umm. That is *obvious.*

But can water multiply? Fluids as a mathematical equation. The terms 'swell' or 'engorge' a more appropriate description. But waterfalls flow *down.* Rain makes the water what? More prolific? Larger? Inflated? What does a waterfall *do*?

It gushes, says Winky. Like you. Now be quiet and enjoy the scenery.

Forget the local attractions in Owaka. Don't bother with the sea lions, the seal colony or even Jack's Blowhole whatever that means. The highlight of Owaka is Teapot Land, a garden hosting a quaint population of teapots surrounding a humble house, its paint peeling from the weatherboard. Above the front door hangs a pink sign cut in the shape of a teapot-man standing on sturdy legs, a Lilliputian curator with grandiose notions, flanked by a scarlet teapot, and a primrose teapot next to a sign saying, 'Closed.' No surprise there. Peer through the windows. Teapots line shelves and window ledges. Outside, a garden and thousands more teapots, perky spouts pointing in opposite directions. Cat, chicken, cow and cottage-shaped teapots, willow patterned teapots on bridges, on pedestals, on patches of mulch, on synthetic grass. Some hang from garden hooks. A totem pole of tin teapots, one on top of the other. A London bus teapot keeps a garden gnome company while he fishes in the oily water of a pond. A wishing well with a moldy roof. A fat ladybug in charge, *Make a wish. Donations. Please Take Photos.* Drop some coins into a waiting teapot. Another sign, *You can count the fairys.* Fairies I think and do not count. Instead admire the slapdash dedication of who does this. A lover of teapots. A fanatic. A teapot reborn as a person. And how to define Teapot Land. A museum or a weapon of exaggeration or a graveyard? Mock seriousness? Teapot burlesque? An allegory? Do the teapots brave extreme weather? Does the owner supply knitted tea cozies during winter? Of course. Teapot Land the happy place. Every ridiculous and pretty object combines generosity and nonsense. Teapots indulge in adventures of their own, shuffling through the garden at midnight, some falling over. Analyze the situation. Observe their imperfections, the cracks, some blemishes. Are they disillusioned with me? My faults, flaws, love handles. And Teapots stare with intense curiosity at me, not understanding the meaning of what I appreciate. Teapot Land catches me off-guard. A surprising lesson, using the qualities of magnification, miniaturization and obsessions. A sweet cluttered vision making me *see* anew. And the important thing. Have a good time. Party. Like the teapots.

On the outskirts of Dunedin, a cardboard sign announces, The Pram Museum. Closed today. Further along an advertisement hammered to a post, Drive-in Radishes, Value For Money. Do they offer a variety? Raw or steamed or grilled? Do the radishes come with French fries and a thick shake? God, I'm hungry.

Winky accelerates.

Hey not so fast. Slow down.

I don't want to stop. There's nothing to do here.

Sometimes that's the best thing to do.

No. It isn't.

The day is early and the wind blows warm, this place grows bean flowers and pea-green grass and swarms of insects hit the high spots, sighing weeds thrive by the road.

We are almost in Dunedin.

Why do *you* want to come to Dunedin?

I don't. You do.

I do not. Whatever gave you that idea? I have no interest in Dunedin. It's your idea.

No. It isn't. It's your idea.

Is not.

Yet somehow we are here. Hungry and laughing and nothing to see.

Dunedin's literary history. Janet Frame, Owls Do Cry. And the albatross lives in Dunedin. Duh. Winky roars,

Instead of the cross, the albatross, around my neck was hung.

Right. What actually is an albatross? I thought they were extinct.

No. That's the Do Do Bird.

Dodo not Do Do.

The royal Albatross, soaring above us, on the windy Taiaroa Head, the Albatross, prince of the clouds searching for prey, the bird laughs at the archer drawing his bow, smiles at stupidity, graceful effortless gliding for hours in the silent sky, but on the ground the Albatross walks like a drunk, and humans jeer at exquisite ugliness all that and more thinks the Albatross ignoring us shivering and stumbling over our beautiful wings below.

South of Dunedin. Wind in our hair. The radio crackling, *Lucy in the sky with diamonds.* My mouth drops open at the sight of a fence strung with hundreds of old shoes, fifty or so yards, beside the driveway, up to a farmhouse. The barbed wire sags from the weight of worn boots, sneakers, gumboots, thongs, slippers and sandals. Winky rubs his eyes.

Well get a load of that disgusting monstrosity. I guess folks around here have a lot of spare time.

You know it might have something to do with sheep.

The farmer's boots disintegrate after years of tromping around after sheep in the mud so he hangs them on his fence. A neighbor visits the farmer one day and decides to hang his wife's slippers on the fence. Every person who happens past follows suit and ties a pair of shoes to the fence. Sort of a chain reaction. And a haven for conformity. This safety of sameness. Consider the habits of sheep, when one sheep faces in a particular direction the remaining flock do the same until lines of sheep face in the same direction. So it goes with the shoes. But without any high heels. Most of the shoes belong to *men.*

A rural town outside Dunedin, two more fences display unique collections. A paling fence, covered in blacks t-shirts, neatly spaced, armless and flattened as if worn by the fence posts. 'TO THE ALL BLACKS!' Several names painted in white on the front of each T-shirt. Nonu 13, Kahui 14, Dagg 15. A complete mystery. Means nothing to me. And on the road to Middlemarch, spot a wire fence constructed completely of rusty old bicycles. A good effort. But not nearly as inspiring or as excellent as millions of filthy shoes, a headless T-shirt named Dagg and the famous brassiere fence in Wanaka, where two hundred bras disappear in broad daylight. Maybe stolen by uptight locals.

Ha! Men don't wear women's underwear.

Some do.

Invercargill, the southernmost westernmost city in New Zealand, lies at the bottom of the world. This town heavily influenced by the Scots and the Presbyterian denomination, the lyrical street names originating from rivers in Scotland; Tyne, Esk, Ness, Yarrow, Spey and Eye. Poetry. With a wide main street, rowdy bars and junk shops, Invercargill could be a Scottish cowboy town. No such thing. Well it's possible. Cowboys in kilts, conjures quite a provocative image and exciting, the prospect of meeting a Scottish cowboy. Become ridiculous. Howdy MacDougall. In tartan chaps and a lasso.

A desolate water tower rises above Invercargill. This structure abandoned by whalers and missionaries and I wonder.

And wander.

About the town. Unearth a copy of The Bobbsey Twins in a junk shop. A notice stuck to a telegraph pole advertises a basilica holding a garage sale. A shop in the center of town offers half price ball gowns. The Robyn Hood Milk Bar stocks dairy, including a range of curd, cream, custard, cheese, cottage cheese, all of it merry.

I am. Keen to gamble, believing the chances of winning are phenomenal in such an underpopulated country. I buy a lottery ticket and win two hundred and forty dollars. I play the pokies and win two hundred and forty dollars interesting odds and I told you so.

Winky keen to try Bluff oysters, searches seafood markets without success. We must go to Bluff, so we drive to Bluff, not much in Bluff, except a wild sea and absent oysters. Windswept a cliff, we can't go any further than Bluff. Winky and Bliss confronting the end of the earth.

Are you happy? We've reached the furthest part of the world. And where do you suppose the oysters went? Eaten by cats. Suicided off the cliff face like lemmings?

Japan. First the whales. Now the oysters.

On the road back to Queenstown, fly past Stu's Fly Shop, Winky brakes and swings the car into Stu's parking lot. He sprints into the shop. Slams the screen door. Oh well whatever. Bliss waits in the car. No clue WTF fishing fly, its occupation, the reason for its existence. Winky raves about superior flys. Willow grubs, trout flys, tackle, beadheads, nymphs, realistic damsels. Suburb names. Superhero steakpie, superhero killer minnow, superhero wee fairy, superhero deadly hero. Glow in the dark. What superb characters for a gay fantasy novel. Winky superhero emerges from the store. Gives me a great smacking kiss. That shop is famous you know. So many fantastic flys. And it's a revelation, how to tie a fly.

Of course it is.

The fact of men excited about the smallest things.

Fields the Color of Cashews

Notes

Tasmania. Lolly shops and fields the color of raw cashews. Roadkill, roos, wombats, even an echidna. A few one-armed people, lots of limpers and curry scallop pies. Glen Clyde house serves orange colored water as pumpkin soup. Velo. Joseph Cromy. Wallaby eating a strawberry. Japanese woman waves goodbye to a man disrobing outside a service station. And that is some extreme.

6

Paris Maybe A Bloody Brilliant Idea

Note

Maybe not.

Christmas ahhh lets get our dreams unstuck and spend a
month in the celestial city of love, city of a hundred villages,
city of lights, La Ville-Lumuire, city of chestnuts lining dusky
boulevards, city of warm baguettes, multi-colored macaroons,
crystal chandeliers, crazy drivers, mulled wine and miserable
force-fed ducks, city of gastronomic grandeur, Coq Au Vin,
paper thin crepes like delicate lace, foie gras on a pedestal,
fricassee escargot and the aroma of a simmering cassoulet,
(nothing more catastrophic than undercooking a cassoulet)
cook in an earthenware pot, sizzle in a pan, this history on a
plate, ooh la la Paris the voluptuous dream, tinting the atmosphere pink and gold, scenting the Seine with desire and regret,
the Seine the color of pewter, here in Paris, the soul takes
a bath of Baudelairian beauty and antique buildings dream

and in their dreams they speak the languages of sunset, soft skies and pure chocolate and a Paris swarming with cupids and marble flesh, her bonbon eyes sparkling at the Manets and Monet's, at shorty Toulouse Lautrec dwarfed and limping from brothel to brothel, at the Eiffel dinosaur, at a café au lait, creme de la crème, Dame Notre duchesse laughing fit to bust, Paris the queen of reveries oh yes and what magic power places her on the throne of deliciousness and pleasure? What what what. It doesn't matter. *Oui.* Paris gives us a kiss on each cheek and says,

There is no place better than me.

A month in Paris. Are you jealous?

Good morning do not wait for the morning. Sings the sound of my voice startling Avenue Du Général Leclerc, my nose flattening against the window pane looking out on a stone church spire across the road and I sing as if sacking a city, trying to elaborate within the prairies of inner silence, shhh, shush the amorous imagination, our chains float on water, life hangs by a thread, we understand nothing and everything.

For we live in an apartment near the meaning of death. The bones of six million Parisians lie just up the road. Don't wake them. This is not for us. We are not comfortable with bones, the idea of dismantled skeletons as thought provoking, true this place of the scary biscuits catacombs, curiosity of kings, jolts our thoughts, a blackbird chirps a warning, shall we go, the queues, so arrive at nine am, second in line, the man in front of us scoots into the caves, but he soon slows for who in their right mind will be alone with this number of bones and eyeless skulls floating without rancor, eyes without hope unable to stare or scold tourists popping the odd skull into a plastic shopping bag.

Romanticize the elsewhere, this passion for listening to a language we do not understand, though Winky linguist extraordinaire adapts his tongue to every country, making himself understood in his flamboyant bowtie, striped shirts and grinning like what else but the Cheshire Cat celebrating the connection, the acceptance, the coherence and the charm of shop assistants and stall owners. Bliss, well, speaks only English. My entire French vocabulary consists of *le la les oui non bonjour bonsoir salute au revoir, mon dieu je ne sais quoi.* And a sentence of German, *Wass iss duss? Duss iss de kugershrieber.* What is this? This is a pen. Duh.

The strange Bliss and strangeness makes sense in France, 'étranger' from another place, not our home, the unfamiliar disguised as familiar our accents giving us away.

On Christmas Eve, the three wisemen or are they Russian spies follow the north star and stop for coffee, will you step inside twinkles the lights and it's snowing and we drink mulled wine *vin chaud* at the Christmas markets and I buy a black beret cliché from a gypsy woman, her hand like a claw boiled in oil. Not a pleasant thought.

And now this last minute search for a turkey in Carrefour's. I imagine the word turkey in French, la turkin or le turk or le turquet. Pretty names. But no la turkins or le turks or le turquets fresh or frozen in this supermarket. Drag Winky away from the wine aisle. Point at what might be a turkey or a chicken, fat from an over-dose of hormones. The word 'chien' printed on the label. Is 'chien' French for turkey? Maybe French for dog, oui it's dog. Hot wine, sweet dynamite on an empty stomach, is that a free sample of brie and the thought of roast dog for Christmas lunch. I feel sick. Winky picks up the shrink-wrapped bird and turns it over.

You will not find murdered refrigerated dogs in a French supermarket. How could you think this.

We must have turkey. The illusive turkey. And sacrifice plum pudding for a Yule log but go on Winky checks his French dictionary. *Dinde.* The French word for turkey. Cue the symphony. *Dinde!* Of course, so logical and such a musical word. Christmas turkey, *dinde de noel.* Stuffed turkey, *blanc de dinde farci.* Turkey stew, *gigolette de dinde.* Shredded turkey, *emince de dinde.* Cold turkey, *sevrage brutal.* Grab the last remaining dinde from the cold food section and toss the bird into the shopping trolley. Sevrage brutal. Head reeling jetlag, chills from the frozen food zone, tipsy from drinking spicy wine, sing under my breath,

Dinde dinde din din diddley din de de la dead dinde divvy up the doddle din din dinde. Going cold turkey. *Sevrage brutal.*

Winky pats my arm,
Are you all right honey?

Now *alors* search the patisserie section for a log. There! The Yule Log a cake or *Buche de Noel* a surreal festive display in Carrefour's. Yule the archaic name for Christmas. Yule Yule Yule! To celebrate the pagan winter solstice. Rejoice! Dance around a bonfire, light candles any candles, sing up the dawn and solstice the longest night, keep vigil until the sun rises at some point, hot damn, the unconquerable sun brings the gift of brilliance and cake and hope.

How to construct the log. Frost roly poly sponge cakes with chocolate butter cream. Urg. Then drag the cream with a fork until it resembles tree bark and it does. Attach a few smaller rolls to the log to look like trimmed branches and they do. Decorate riotously with spun sugar cobwebs, sprigs of marzipan holly,

meringue mushrooms, candy pot-bellied Santa's, plastic rein-
deers and snowmen wearing scarves and bowler hats. Sprinkle
the whole shebang with sugar snow and don't overdo it.

A black and white street sign says, Aston Martin Parking
Only. All Other Cars Will Be Crushed. My god where are
we? The deep south condemning cars to death, the fact of
segregation, discrimination and capital punishment for cars,
Aston Martin supremacy. This concept of superior cars and
inferior cars hey complex oh these complexes what a to
do. The helpless and dependent car, the imperfection, the
rust, the dents, the lack of ambition, the lack of self-esteem
and social contact, all other cars, every car in the world will
be crushed, will feel crushed. Oh but the supreme Aston
Martin, its exaggerated pretentions of cringeworthy who do
you think you are, haughty vain bragging about its shine
and trimmings. The Aston Martin indulging in tyrannical
behavior *All Other Cars Will Be Crushed. Mais c'est* normal.
Don't worry about it.'

I fill our Paris apartment with flowers. Flowers make my
heart beat faster, a good thing, not like the toilet, the size,
one square meter, like a dog kennel but with a high ceiling.
Poor Winky must poop with the door open and his feet in the
hallway. Not a pretty sight. Look at the flowers.

Notre Dame, on the opposite side of the Seine, shines a
luscious orange through leafless trees under soft grey clouds
and the palest hint of a china sky. At sunset. So there.

So poetic.

Poetic! This reading French poetry. The Eel Pie, The
Dressmaker, The Ear-Maker and The Mould-Mender, The
Glutton, The Falcon, The Magnificent, The Impossible Thing,

The Hermit, The Sick Abbess, The Truckers, The Pack-Saddle, The Old Man's Calendar, The Kiss Returned.

In Paris, a poodle seems appropriate, like the lady with the little dog walking along the Pont-Neuf, the lady in black, of course a diamond dog collar and lead and the little dog barks and the lady barks, they both bark in French *oeuff oeuff oeuff* and Notre Dame nods approval.

Pont-Neuf, the most romantic place in the world, hugs our starry eyes, say, love you, embrace below the rows of ornate iron street lamps lining the bridge, aloof lamps radiating a superiority complex, lamps glaring down at me and saying,

We are taller, fancier and much more elegant than you in your cheap beret and clodhopping fur-lined boots.

In every other city except Paris, the rain smells stale, but in Paris, the rain turns into rose scented mist. Do you believe this.

Before Christmas, suggest a visit to Sarah and Declan, friends of mine living in Wokingham. Sarah and Declan are such *fun*. When they were living in New York they smoked crack cocaine and didn't realize what it was until years later. We'll catch the cross channel ferry, leave early Saturday morning, get there in time for dinner, ahh sweet optimism, Paris to Calais, a three and a half hour train trip, and the ferry from Calais to Dover. Simple.

We wait at Gare de Calais-Ville, a deserted station, quite a distance from the ferry terminal. We wait knee deep in snow, with eight or more silent people of darting eyes, sense suspicion, a woman wears a Mickey Mouse hat, woolen scarves hide double chins, no sign of impatience, not far from Gallipoli, not a cab in sight, no one speaks. Are there taxis in Calais or a bus from the station to the ferry, here we are stranded in the snow like baby seals that lost their mother, quite sure if a taxi appears we will all club each other to death. A middle-aged couple (Australian) sun damaged skin, hideous haircuts, nylon anoraks stare at Winky and me as if we are vermin. Maybe there's a shuttle bus. No timetable. No buses to the ferry terminal. No hope. It begins to rain. We start to walk to the ferry terminal. Plenty of time. Haul my suitcase with frozen wheels. Plod through snow banks and slush for almost an hour. Winky chooses the longest route down Rue De La Mare and we turn right onto Boulevarde de la Resistance, Bliss whining all the way, what the fuck.

Ferry terminal, the size of a small planet. Check in. At one o'clock, Winky and Bliss collapse onto plastic chairs in the terminal café. Remember the meaning of terminal, fatal, incurable, deadly, life-threatening, lethal. Our ferry due to depart at two pm. The intercom announcing delays in several languages. Now. Departure at three. I text Sarah, *ferry running late, stuck in Calais won't make it until sixish.* In the café, waiting for the call, the meaning of delay, suspension, stoppage, setback, re-schedule. And this feeling of constipation occurs. On the way to the restroom, a surge of people appear, running up the stairs and hundreds and hundreds of travelers pour into the café. My usual panic, is this some sort of Eastern European invasion? Run back to Winky, ah precious sipping on his Pilsner. Oblivious to the ever-increasing crowd.

Winky look at all these people.

Something's up. We better get on the next ferry.

People start rushing down the stairs. We run with them. First to the ticket office. Then the bus. No. Wrong bus. Scuttle back to the ticket office. This group of us becomes an entity, a mass of which way to go, over there, run to the other bus. Christ. We aren't even on the ferry yet. Thousands more people materialize, everyone looks desperate. I remember the deserted town, no taxis or buses, the struggle through the snow to the terminal. Where do all these people come from and how are they here?

Chaos on the ferry. Pushing and shoving, a sort of polite violence. We search for a quiet spot to sit. Fries, popcorn, ketchup, crisp packets litter the floors and tables, the corridors full of screaming children, raucous couples, loud music, poker machines and blaring televisions. Eager for beer, Winky trots over to the bar and disappears into a throng of burly yobs. Bliss sits in a booth and prepares myself for the last thing in world I want, only an hour and a half of hell and maybe Dover, the destination, the sanity of England, hale and hearty. The table near me speaks and I eavesdrop. Two men introducing themselves to a young woman.

Hi I'm Owen and this is Ivan. Isn't this crazy? Were you on the Eurostar? We've been trapped in a tunnel for sixteen hours. Four Eurostar trains broke down in the tunnel on Friday night. The power went. Us and the other passengers stayed on the train overnight without light, air conditioning, food or water. People fainted with claustrophobia and asthma attacks, children slept on the floor, some were sick, others urinated in the aisles.

Ivan and Owen boast how they opened the emergency doors and escaped, stumbling through the blackness and live cables in search of refuge in another train.

I text Sarah, *bit of a crisis here won't make it until sevenish.*

Winky plunks a glass of wine in front of me, lifeline wine, elixir of the patron saint of travel, save us drink faster than my whole life, will this help the situation. Winky's expression of thunderous.

You and your ideas. Pop over to London for the weekend. Why not pop over to a war zone.

Weren't we hugging the day before on the Pont Neuf, the romance, it's not my fault, blame the Eurostar breaking down. One of the French train drivers locking himself in the engine room and crying. What a sook. People suffocating completely traumatized break the doors open. Eurostar evacuating two thousand passengers the next morning and canceling all their services and everyone sent to Calais.

Dover. A calamitous crush, shoulder to shoulder, clawing, us and them of the determine eyes, me first, me first, desperation gives way to selfish shoves, the tunnel of their furor, have to be somewhere important, cramming onto the buses, us in the middle, hang on to each other, never let me go, a hand in one of Winky's pockets, not my hand.

Hey! Someone just went through my pockets.

Give him a nudge.

Sshh, you sound like a crazy person.

He elbows several people and bellows,

Someone just tried to rob me.

Get on the bus. You're embarrassing me.

Such a big coach to take us the short distance to the bus terminal, to incoherence in Dover, surprise no buses to the train station, about a thirty minute walk from the terminal, argh all along the road, people trudge, hunching from the cold, dragging their suitcases and Winky and I follow them. I text Sarah,

Stuck in Dover won't make it until nineish.

Oh God they booked their favorite restaurant. Hope the trains run on time. We change for Wokingham at Paddington. Right?

Soldier on, am I losing weight, am I losing my sanity, my mind functions as if injected with gelatin, drag my bag slipping here and there, how far is the station, why build it there, oh it's always been there, before the ferry terminal the size of an Olympic stadium. A song, I don't really know appears of course *Walk on through the wind, Walk on through the rain. Walk on, walk on, With hope in your heart,* Winky wait for me, he slows down, we're nearly there, am I breathing.

On the train to London, I remember a man on the train with wild black hair and a bony face gorging on fish and chips from butcher's paper and how hungry I am and the sordid sight of him eating with his mouth open and his fanatical eyes and us in our daze of not understanding the enormity of the transport problem. Not knowing that fifty-five thousand people are stranded in Paris and London and the only way in and out is by ferry.

Eleven pm. Arrive at Sarah and Declan's. Apologize. Declan is drunk, more wine? Yes please. More wine. Spend a few hours chatting. A tired Sarah also tipsy, confessing he's just a filthy old man. Marriage in tatters. House a bombsite. Piles of washing in the laundry reaching the top of the dryer. Drinking another glass of wine, Sarah says,

I'm working full time now. Declan home all day ignores the housework. He doesn't want to go on holiday. He just sits around the house reminiscing about the sixties in London. He smells. I can't bear to be near him. Oh and he can't get it up anymore. The frustration is killing me, so I bought a vibrator.

Gulps a glass of wine and tops up mine.

Oh God I shouldn't complain at least we still have this house even Though we lost all our money in the crash. Hey we no longer have the guest room. We threw out the sofa bed and I've furnished the room with gym equipment

We clear a path to a mattress on the floor in their teenage daughter's bedroom. Clothes, books, cosmetics and rubbish strewn on chairs and over the rug of we will survive, they will too, a marvelous future, they have this house on the river and a pool and a cruiser and wine. Winky whispers,

I thought you said Declan and Sarah were *fun*.

People change.

Yes they do.

Sunday morning five am. Skip breakfast. Catch the train back to London and then another train to Dover. Trudge from Dover station to the ferry terminal again, but in reverse, without a cup of tea or a bowl of cereal, the pangs of a futile visit and arriving back at this gateway to Europe, amazing no one about, a lukewarm sun shining hopefulness renews, faith, put this hideous weekend behind us, race back to Paris, the fastest way, oh right the ferry, wishing me dead, but for the hope of been through the worst of it, will not get any worse, until we are in Paris, the English channel swimmable for god's sake and we enter through the glass doors of the Passenger Services Building to complete and utter pandemonium. Winky's eyes bulge.

Oh my sweet sainted aunt.

Hundreds of people desperate to book a ticket to Calais. Three operators and queues not even queues, but masses pushing at every counter.

Not to worry we have our tickets.

The confidant 'don't mess with me' side of Winky approaches a security guard and asks directions to board the ferry. The security guard, slippery chap with a hairy slug above his top lip, snaps his heels together, do they practice that tone completely devoid of emotion.

You are required to check in at the counter sir. I can't allow you to board sir. Ticket or no ticket, sir, everyone must check in at the counter.

That's just sheer bloody mindedness. We already bought tickets. Please allow us to board.

The guard lifts his chinless. Assumes the expression of, there is nothing I can do about it.

Those are the rules sir.

Dash back to the ticket counter just as one of the operators shuts down his computer and exits the building. The tangled mass of people breathe in collective rage. The counters now twenty deep with this jostling angry crowd. Winky edges into the mob. I squash onto a jam-packed bench. Put our bags between my feet. And way over there on the other side of the room. Might be a café, but for my eyesight and if it is a café, shall I leave the bags, push my way through the crowd? The cafe might not be a café. The café might be closed. Or run out of coffee. I spiral into a void. Winky gets nearer to the ticket seller. Inch by inch, three people in front of him and after forty-five minutes, a wild-eyed Winky back by my side,

We are officially checked in and now we can board.

We fly up an escalator into a windowless corridor and another endless queue. A real queue. A queue of resignation. The willpower to muddle through and be optimistic flies away on wings of godforsaken we just can't take this anymore. This is not where I want to die.

We should have bought a bottle of water.

Winky looks grim.

Too late now. Nobody allowed back in the terminal.

Fatal incurable deadly life-threatening hopeless starvation this then the meaning of stranded. In front of us, a jolly French family unwrap a packed lunch of juice boxes, potato crisps and baguettes filled with salad. We open our books. Sit on our bags for the love of oblivion and read in a coma-like state, time slows. We wait in the queue for nine hours. Beyond hunger. Dehydration. The idea of peeing laughable. I finish reading Infinite Jest.

Nine o'clock, we board the ferry, crumple in a quiet corner, wonder about the availability of. Winky dashes to the bar for food and drink. My hero. Anything to sustain life. Something strong. Returns with wine and two inedible Cornish pasties. Which we devour.

All they had. Got into a fight with the barman.

What do you mean? A fist fight?

No. I asked for another pasty. He sneered, only one pasty per passenger. Can you believe it? I told him to go to hell.

Winky cramming the dry pasty into his mouth, the flakey and a 'god only knows' mush stuffing and then I dream of Winky like a Wild West cowboy lunging over the bar and punching the barman full in the face.

We are not very good travelers are we?

Three hours, a black sea, howling winds, phoning hotels in Calais, everything booked, no room at the inn, these few days before Christmas, how a wise person loses its way.

Midnight, arrive in Calais. No taxis. Fellow passengers greet family and friends whisking them away in heated cars to fires and cognac and hugs and kisses I imagine, and not one of them offer the stranded passengers a lift to the train station, a five minute drive, those selfish uncaring French, they must have seen the hundreds of us standing hopefully in the snow and slush. When will this nightmare be over, this slush pile, now refugees. A staff member offers us a choice. Sleep in the terminal or be transported to a nearby facility. Ah horror the prospect of spending the night on a plastic chair in the ferry terminal. Choose the facility oh maybe an asylum, a sanitorium, a death camp things will not get any worse. A coach pulls up. The stranded ones board weary wishful thinking in the darkness and silence through the sleeping town avoid braking, that screech on streets of heavy eyelids, keep the lid on, am I dreaming this, when will we wake. The bus drops us at a school sports center. Local Red Cross volunteers distribute army blankets, cold sandwiches and bottles of water donated by a supermarket. Do we feel hungry. Hunger, thirst, basic needs, refrigerated bread, can't keep my eyes open, do we speak in this crowd of about four hundred people asleep on camp beds on the floor of the gymnasium of prone and hunch and snore anonymous bodies. Winky finds a space under the basketball hoops. Halos at least lie down on the floor, wrap myself up in the thick felt blanket. Fall asleep. Winky of course doesn't sleep a wink.

Four o'clock in the morning, we are up, we gather, we queue, we bedraggle, how far to the station. In the snow. One bus arrives to eight hundred eyes, blank stares are they stupid, we a total of millions, shall we sit on laps, we have all slept together without looking or speaking, not even good morning, how did you sleep, well badly I slept on the floor. Only the elderly and mothers with children to go first. To the station. A British man standing behind us groans, blimey. I remember how unruffled his appearance is, as if his wife has only just ironed his pants, the seams straight, dying to get to his holiday house in Provence, he tells us, I have a holiday house in Provence, nice, we reply, we are staying in Paris, he makes a suggestion.

Pretend to be elderly.

We are kind of, old, but well, definitely middle-aged, okay fake a limp. And Winky deranged by now, dodders up to the bus driver and shouts,

We are elderly.

Both of us so disheveled and un-ironed, the driver waves us onto the bus.

In the Paris apartment, a temporary home, cups of sweet tea and sleep in a proper bed and what happened dreaming a nightmare, the exhaustion, on the point of death, stay put, keep within the perimeters of Paris until the very last. Do you realize we caught the train from Calais to Paris a day late and sat in first class all the way to Gare De Nord and not one ticket collector ever asked us for our tickets.

The Tiniest Balls Of Foam Imaginable

Notes

Madrid. Neck cushion. Grand bazaar glory times. Waiter pronounces wifi wee fee. Old man in purple beret babbling. Navalcarnero Mostoles Segovia. Alcoa. 159405 kilometers. Cafe with chips, chips principe, chips novella, sticks and orbit gum. Rubbish bins with tiny windows attached to light poles in the streets. Old man in a parakeet beanie has a look, reaches in, pulls out some crumpled tin foil, nothing in there. Madrilenos on zebra crossings. Snowflakes like the foam in the neck support. Dinner at Sobrino De Botin the oldest restaurant in the world. Chipped hand-painted plates on the wall. Pen and ink drawings of the room we are in. Five framed certificates on the wall. Suckling pig. Guitar player strumming and singing, 'here comes the sun and I say it's alright.' A piano accordion plays, 'wake me up before you go go.' The Prado hello Hieronymus! Happy days in The Garden of Earthly Delights and scores of crucified Christs with neat amounts of blood spurting from slits shaped like lips just below his ribcage. And dark

Goyas' lifted from the walls of his house in Madrid all about the brushstrokes deft and swift. And the grotesque facial expressions, he departs from the usual sickly colors. Cars named Duster. Twingo, a six story building selling low cost show girls. We argue in front of the apartment building, where to catch a cab. Graveyard just outside Madrid. Nespresso machine in the apartment. Regia Sofia cafeteria, my shoes match the dark red chrome ceiling. In italics, on the side of a multi-story building, this sign saying, In The Dissected Fruit Of My Mirror. Song playing in the physiotherapist, I face the final curtain I did what I had to do I saw it through without exception I did it my way. Corkscrew in Spanish. Saca Corchero. Nowhere to be found. Cobblestone squares Don Quixote. Short woman at the chicken shop. The young people, happy to practice their English. Others, very unfriendly short-legged and glum. Where are the high combs and mantillas? And in the countryside, the risks. Boulders scattered yet arranged and stone walls curve over hills where trees have fallen.

Travel the thirty hours from Sydney to London that Australians are so familiar with, this journey to Europe and I think how sadistic of the airline staff to create this schedule where first thing in the morning bedraggled Australian bodies, stuck in a different time zone of three or four in the morning, slap myself in the face, boarding a plane at Heathrow along with fresh faced well-dressed Brits and Spanish commuters hopping a flight to Madrid.

And as we land.

Bliss capable of unknown decisions, rips the label off my neck pillow filled with the lightest tiniest balls of foam imaginable. Makes a big hole in the seam. Tiny balls of foam spurt out with surprising intensity, some airborne, the rest disperse over clothes, the floor, the seats. Balls with fierce tenacity, cling to everything, fly over the seats, flecks land on headrests, invade my nostrils, nestle in the dark hair of a man across from us. Unbelievable the amount of foam in one of those pillows. Try brushing it off. Winky wakes up in my accidental snowstorm, foam in his hair, clinging to his eyebrows and floating around his face. Flaps his hands. Disrupts more foam.

My God Bliss, what have you done?

Why do I do the things I do. I shove the exploding pillow under the seat and sneeze. The cabin doors open. Passengers file out. Winky and Bliss, the last ones up the aisle, leave behind an ethereal trail of the ghastly stuff.

Four weeks in wintry Madrid. This mountain city marooned on a rocky tableland. Heat and cold comes and goes quickly like a tempestuous love affair. Interpret grey Spanish skies as we miss the city's most splendid asset, the famous light and sunshine. But choose winter in Madrid. Because they describe the summer as nine months of hell.

Madrid is a woman from Chamberi, short with permed hair colored a dirty blonde, and dresses the same as all the other women, in a mid-calf length fur coat, tailored black trousers and a silk scarf, tottering with her hand through her pint-sized husband's arm, both of them together for many years, never been apart, both leaning on walking sticks held by gloved hands, he wears the same dapper jacket and peaked cap as the other older men prefer city life to the harshness of the countryside and their height and outfit match each other perfectly as they stroll arm in arm through the somber rhythm of a day out.

A spacious apartment on Calle Hilerion in quaint Chamberi, this neighborhood of an older generation, urban beings of a stubborn mindset.

An old man wearing a purple beret, as if he got up that morning and put on his usual dull jacket and pants and then a radical thought strikes him. He decides to wear his purple beret. Someone might notice him. Somebody does.

Siesta, a little night in the middle of the day, this instinctive and vital ingredient of human enjoyment, the shops close, we have to get up earlier, you mean you have to get up earlier, for as if by magic the streets are deserted until six or seven pm and then the metal shutters sealing shop fronts, roll up in expectation.

Leave the apartment at a sensible hour and miss my step and twist my knee badly. I can't walk without a stick so I join the throng of Spaniard's walking with sticks. At least I'm not the only one.

But I can't go far and as we have swapped cars as well as homes, we decide to drive most places. The owners of the apartment left written instructions,

The car. To get there: where you take the Metro Moncloa, there is also a bus station, take bus No. 627 (in Isla -1) to Villanueva de la Canada. Your stop is the last one in Villanueva, it is in front of a building with gold aluminum windows. Call beforehand and Sven will pick you up and will give you the car. V. de la Canada is a thirty to forty minute ride in the bus from the bus station in Moncloa. It is a pleasant journey and rarely crowded on the bus.

Is this the bus to Villanueva de la Canada?

The bus driver sneers and demands our tickets, then refuses to sell us tickets and shuts the automatic bus door in our faces. Three buses go through the terminal while purple-faced Winky bolts from one end to the other trying to buy bus tickets, which we then discover can be bought on the bus. Finally on our way, the bus driver floors the accelerator and drives like a car rally contestant for the whole forty minute journey to Villanueva de la Canada, a featureless modern residential municipality west of Madrid. We meet Sven and he gives us the keys to this sturdy Pajero, an old jalopy lovingly preserved, equipped with huge bumper bar that proves adequate in dealing with the mad Spanish drivers. We fail to locate the building with the golden windows.

In the city, we soon discover the locals have some sort of death wish. Without acknowledging the four-wheel drive not quite speeding, but going at a fair clip through the city streets, a pedestrian, without looking right or left, steps suddenly onto the zebra crossing. Winky slams on the brakes and I scream. This happens ten or so times every day for the rest of our time in Madrid prompting me to shriek,

Watch out, stop stop, you're going to hit that bloke, Winky for Christssake slow down.

Our nerves shattered, we almost wipe out half the aged population of Madrid, as yet another person, without skipping a beat, steps blindly onto a busy road and all the cars either screech to a halt or swerve around them.

Cookie Crisis

Notes

Budapest. Try to forget the toilet on the train to Budapest. The battle scars of pockmarked buildings. The thermal spa stinks. A combination of the baroque and one flew over the cuckoo's nest Worst massage from an enormous girl. Felt exhilarated over the next few days when the minerals took hold. In Budapest folk lore, pagans push a bishop in a barrel lined with nails over a cliff. Two dogs walking unaccompanied. The three cookies. Madame, I have some terrible news. A supermarket named Albert. A town called Kolin. Butterflies painted on a brick tower.

In a Budapest café, across the road from the synagogue, the grimy plastic menu has individual pictures of three cookies. I point to the cream centred chocolate cookie. The young waiter brings my coffee and says,

Madame, I have some terrible news.

I imagine the Russian army amassing on the border. The waiter continues,

I am compoundly sorrowful. Please understand Madame, it seems we have only one type of cookie today.

My panic subsides and he indicates the vanilla cookie is available.

On the night ferry ride, the gold palaces and cathedrals, a bridge arcs of light strung delicately below dots of light dancing above black water.

I spend two hours trying on hats and purchase the saucer hat, a fitted cap with stripes on a round piece the size of a dinner plate and a thick black felt hat puffy like a mushroom, the mushroom hat. I do not know where will I wear them, not in this heat and hot and exhausted, I leave the shopping bag with my two hats on a park bench, thinking I am still carrying the bag. Ghost hats. The loss brings the capacity for regret, for blame, for fretting, but also the hope some woman finds my hats and takes pleasure in wearing them, while I waste my energy, which is invisible and not worth spurting about like a geyser.

In the Synagogue, I know the dead know we are here visiting, remembering and we'll never forget their deaths. And the Jewish ghetto, the weight of past pain inconceivable, the acts unthinkable, a time without mercy and thousands visit to bring back the light, to remember their souls are whole and here and knowing.

A labyrinth of grungy hipster bars. The atmospheric Szimpla Kert, (simple garden) a ruin bar transforms a tenement house. A cave entrance a tavern space with a cannibalized old Trabant car in the middle, like an eclectic junk yard, rubbish in a good way, decorated with collages, peeling shutters, sets of skis, old post office signs, sawn off mannequins, wire netting, dismembered dolls, light fittings made of waste paper baskets, bare light bulbs, old computers, sewing machines, stuffed rabbits and toys on swings hanging from the ceiling. Miles of wires and fairy lights criss-crossing the ceiling. There are carrots on the menu, nasty mojitos and plenty of shisha.

Italy. Genova. Safety belts in the train. Wallpaper in the train. Bitters rosemary, Statue of a king holding a pumpkin. Uffizi. Baroncelli. Portrait of Maria Bonciani looks like Meryl Streep. Sign on a hill 'baby frattoria.' Rome. In the middle of a zebra crossing, a round man bouncing a soccer ball on his head. Boy punching the girl in front of him at the Colosseum. Gah. Rose petals in the basilica. Bologna. Junkie in the shoe shop. Farting priest in San Antonio. Kuwaiti hooker on the train to Venice. One legged pigeons. Skulls with bows.

Czech. A cuckoo clock on the train to Prague. The Kafka museum. Korean girl singing Ave Maria on Palacky Bridge.

Berlin. The giant key. The Jewish renaissance. Turnip soup at the New National Museum. Hartnackschule means happy hour.

Toledo. Flamenco music in the underground car park. Fish sellers beside the Teatroderojas. Man with chartreuse hair, flaming ruby goatee, white socks. A child steals my wallet and a woman returns it to me minus cash, before I realize it is stolen. The confusion then.

Valencia. A field of purple cabbages.

Córdoba. Woman at breakfast with murderous red hair like a palm tree on fire.

Cuenta. Drive-thru coffee from McDonalds, a tray with extra espressos in paper cups and sticks for stirrers. Storks nesting on the tops of towers.

Ronda. Carmona bike riding into Seville. Three tails attached to a black bag. What is a rio tinto sign? It's wavy lines.

Portugal. Posada de Tavira Convention da Graca, Rua Dom Paio Peres Correia. Seafood restaurant. A man spends twenty minutes choosing wine. Thump is mashed potato. Pull up in front of the convent and an elfin train chugs around the corner. March is the month of Gambrinus, chickpea stew. Head north Rua de Prata left to Almada. Continue into Sao Domingus right onto Portus Santo Antao.

7

Sweatenings

Sri Lanka. Buddhist retreat. Staff choir singing in the dining hall. Send email from the lobby of a perspiring like some sort of unknown species, bandit mosquitoes, forty five minutes to log on, write email, before I press send. Total power failure. We don't mention money here. Pay the bill in secret. A smiley face, 'thank you for appreciating our work' on the front of a sturdy tip box beside a tin of Diamond white oats. Woman glaring, silence please. This place in time, men wear skirts and thick silver rings. Mangos and an orange fish nose pokes out of the pond. If I re-read this I remember paying the bill and free nights and strange red paper lanterns and how the ceiling fan dries my sweat and how worried I am the ceiling fan in the room might decapitate me. A chipmunk nesting in the outdoor speaker. The German man says to me you are sweatening too. Perspiration rivers riv-ering…

Pomegranates float quiet in the pool. A greed crow perching on the carcass of an elephant drifts down a river. Greedy and innocent. Water lilies crowd the koi slipping orange fins and silver scales of fish mouths nipping mosquitos.

The wise find more than is lost. There wisdom flutters a perhaps stare of question, why do we fall into a frightful one hundred and forty-five hells and invite suffering like a frog transfixed by a walking stick?

Somebody tell me all the why away

beyond where just so and so

enough, the far-remove of a thing

what a silent, somebody tell me.

Spring here, careful monsoon soon. Mangos and blossoms fall in the why not. Well. If one commits evil deeds and is reborn as a ghost the throat remains parched with not even snot or phlegm to drink. Urk yuk blah.

Do you notice. Chipmunks nesting in the outdoor speakers. Religion commands, serve as if a doormat for rubbing feet on. A shiny snake slithers across my path. Keep your virtue as pure as moonbeams, protect it like the yak its tail, win to the bliss of release.

But think. Give yourself a variety of dancing and prancing, going about in a putrid body until ferocious death comes to snatch you away, instead. Express adoration worshipful devotion for the incomparable tamer of the untamable, ask your tamer to allow you to have the last word.

Now Is Not The Time To Be Different
(story)

What I pack. Sarongs, sandals, sunhat blew off and. A razor.
Bring one pair of old underpants any what. There experience
a heavenly bliss of emancipation from. Any old. Here sharpen
your dull. Polish the self. Whet your sing of. Thoughts raging
mine. Thinking of a million ways to die.

A bronze woman wound with a silk sari edged in gold.
Her golden skin, tiny sag of love handles and a belly exposed
like a ginger pudding. She purrs.

Welcome Madam.

She hands me a carved pineapple. Mmmm big and heavy
wood I am asking her.

What's this?

Your room key Madam.

The room built by forever of white stucco and timeless
timber bedhead hung with netting and a view of the reef at a
biteable distance. Hello waves remember the tsunami in a rush

of killings so, now is not the time to be different. Now is not. Different is not the time now. Now is the time to be Healthy. Be Healthy any song. How health find here at The Dharma-sangamaJihimaDighaanGut Health Retreat.

She holds up two smooth stones. As large as alone and the second the shape of a kidney.

Choose.

Can I have both.

She gives me her disapproval. She blinks her healthy glow. Of lowering eyes-always-smile. Guess what? Tell her.

I have a horrible rash.

A religious leader claims true fabrication fabricates the mind of look unhappy. What else can a rash be. Keep it a fester. Symbolizes golly gosh gee Me. Be brave for. And the sun like sex comes up-up-up into the open of every pretty. *Go on.* Throw the world a tongue lash. Hey do not indulge in this frivolous talk. Frivolity leads anyone the royal road to hell. Hells bells. Oh that. Grunt-grit stamping queer whistle chump chomping Rage. Rings a bell.

Silence please.

Finger to her lips as. Every flower blooms without a sound. Pomegranates float quiet in the pool. A greed crow perches on the carcass of an elephant drifting down a river.

I shave my pubes and under my arms. The rash spreads to my armpits itches. By the by. Wishing for the haves, the musts for a cure. Threw my wishes at has anybody seen?

The sign in the dining hall. *We love our animals but let's refrain from inviting them to the bedroom.*

The day she takes me by the hand.

Come Madam.

We walk past the pond. Life. Water lilies crowd the koi slipping orange fins and silver scales. Fish mouths bob and nip mosquitos. The wise find more than is lost. There wisdom flutters a perhaps stare of question. Why do we fall into a frightful one hundred and forty-five hells and invite suffering like a frog transfixed by a walking stick? Somebody tell me all the. Why away beyond where. Just so and so enough. The end of a piece of thing what a marvel the silent string. I mean. Spring here careful monsoon soon.

Here Madam.

Oily massages melt me. Smelly poultices infiltrate the. Steamings ring my layers of moisture. Herbal baths submerge and. Fine needles insert into skin, scalp, wrist, stomach. Where most must needs jabbing. I am a body of meat basted, marinated, roasted, steamed, skewered. Anything glistening greater alive.

The rash redder creeps over my nipples. I am. I smear ointment. Fuck it. Cruel flesh. The itch tears at me. I haven't any why.

Mangos and blossoms fall in the why not. Well. If one commits evil deeds and is reborn as a ghost the throat remains parched with not even snot or phlegm to drink. Urk yuk blah.

The rash spreads to my navel. And I worry the ceiling fan will snap and decapitate me.

Drink this Madam.

Ten swallows of thick oil and bitter herbs from a glass cup. *Urrgh.*

Walk for an hour Madam. Rest every ten minutes Madam. Go to your room and wait Madam.

What for.

Your inside will be cleaned Madam.

Anticipation wonders mop and broom. In My Room. Until. Urgent thunderous roars from gut. A bullet train, upside down volcano, liquid dynamite, high pressure hose. I think high speed panic. The rash disappears as if in fright of a head-on crash. And I shit the world. I sweat an ocean. I retch living creatures. Night and dress me as the universe I am ready to die. She brings me a bowl of broth.

Did you go Madam?

Where.

Stool.

Yes.

How many times Madam?

Eight.

And the vomit.

I hurled like a hungover prom queen.

I do not understand Madam.

Yes. I vomited.

The cleanse is complete Madam.

Great. What next.

Enema Madam.

I die clean again in the whitewashed room. Do you notice. Chipmunks nesting in the outdoor speakers. Religion commands, you must serve as a doormat for rubbing feet on. A shiny snake slithers across my path. Keep your virtue as pure as moonbeams, protect it like the yak its tail, win to the Bliss of Release. But I think. You give yourself a variety of dancing and prancing. You going about in a putrid body until ferocious death comes to snatch you away. Instead. Express adoration worshipful devotion for the incomparable tamer of the untameable. Ask your tamer to allow you to have the last word. Ok.

How about the last word?

No Madam.

Listen there's an extraordinary universe next door.

You are not the same as other people are you Madam.

Well. No.

I see a beach boy take a leak. I hear a girl scream like a parrot. I find mud in the toilet. I watch a grasshopper swoon. I fear we are all morons.

Speak for yourself Madam.

Oh, I do.

Bargain for the night to squeeze the day. You see.

I am not the same as anyone and. We are all killing ourselves in different ways.

Now is not the time to be different, Madam.

Benevolence and Simplicity In China

Notes

Go to pig places and don't know how we get there. Today inside a poem while researching whatever and well now I know medieval infertile men ate ground pig's testicles and the Chinese found 2800 dead pigs in the Huangpu River in 2013 and that tens of thousands of other pigs in China died of swine flu, no reports on how those carcasses were disposed leads me to The Pig poem.

China, the great rice basket, the great leap forward, great! Struggle sessions, not so great, sort of party-orchestrated public struggle and criticism sessions, more struggle, I struggle naturally without meaning too.

Ruin culture being the destruction of old habits old customs, old ideas, burn the books, bury the scholars, destroy everything that matters to an individual, to me, but what matters to me doesn't matter, because it only matters to me and I often come up with impractical ideas and I cannot eliminate my disastrous habits, one being laziness, which makes me a hopeless communist, but fortunate in not being born post-revolution in China and seeing the forced destruction of beauty.

The ghost towns, polluted rivers, a population of faceless numbers.

This country of unwanted daughters, 'you are only a girl, you are spilt water.' In the past, Heroine Mothers give birth to ten or more children and receive an award, what the, a red rosette. If I give birth to ten children I'd like a million dollars.

Then somehow this culling, the temporary measure of the one-child policy, evil or necessary or both, can I ask the female population how do you feel about the state owning a woman's ovaries, fallopian tubes and womb, parts of your body do not belong to you even though they are inside you and somehow, I decide this might be a kind of poetry as tragedy and I hate that idea and the fact of wrapping fetuses in black plastic bags leaving them in communal dustbins and that doctors sell healthy newborns half-price and selling babies in batches. Let me buy them all. And family planning monitors rummage through rubbish checking for soiled sanitary napkins. So, what do you do for a living? When you find what you are looking for then what?

The change. Now, Government slogans claim 'Girls Are As Good As Boys.' 'Girls Are Good.' 'Boys And Girls Are Both Treasures' 'Boy Or Girl? Permit Nature to Decide.'

The Chinese call Westerners 'hairy long noses.' Which sounds creepy and I hear the sound of sniffing. Am I deformed? With an extended nose. Do my sapphire eyes spook the Chinese?

Ninth day of the eighth lunar month. Think about the question of burning. How the Chinese wave burning money over ancestral graves on Tomb Sweeping Day. There will be no point in time where I burn money.

Chinese people with a weak constitution take part in such activities as willow planting, tug-o-war, stepping-the-green outgoing not sure what that is and rooster fighting. I find. Roosters terrifying.

In my heart and mind, China! Shall we, it's your idea, then write it down, in private, on a piece of paper, what else will I write it on, scratch it into a tree trunk, chalk on a pavement, be practical oh you know writing the question down helps to dwell on the question to avoid ambiguity, my question, anyone explain, what, the question of are you sure, the wording of your question must require clarification for example, why am I lost, do not ask a question that requires a 'yes' or 'no' answer, this question of, why am I here, where shall I go, ask what if or what is this all about, I think I ask this on a previous occasion and not a suggestion, more of a command.

Let's Fly To Shanghai.

Winky and Bliss emperor and peasant, scholar and unlearned. Why. Does it matter. Toss three coins in the air. For countless centuries these eerie divinations of the I Ching. We go. Name us after two Chinese literary characters, Benevolence (Winky) and Simplicity (Me) fly to anyway maybe Shanghai seek to understand timeless wisdom and whatever questions sit on our hearts.

Yielding.

Wing me to heaven above, wing us to China below with earth above, earth below, the receptive earth in power, Simplicity follows the natural path of calmness and correct persistence.

On the flight to Shanghai, I read a novel, a doorstep kind of book. Thick. A suburban drama about partners, spouses and kids at a birthday backyard barbeque where a parent slaps a child who is not one of his children, resulting in everyone pissed off, a fallout destabilizing the lives of. So only slap the children in Australia, for Chinese children are spilt water. Bow down to the boys. Throw the girls in the trash. Cry for them lost and read about slapping to try not to think about tragedy and poetry and auctioning ovaries, fallopian tubes and wombs to the highest bidder.

A bump. Christ. Only thunderclouds indicate profound disquiet. Undertake no distant goal, for instance acquiring the power to move objects without touching them, to discover curious rain, the time it rains stickleback fish, frogs, lizards, slate rain, gold rain, to witness the day wheat rains down on peasants.

Concern yourself with the problems of the moment. But a simple woman dreams as spring water collects the heaven above, water below, conflict, heaven and water, strength and profundity, conflict, avoid confrontation, yield with caution, persist not against obstacles, at the base of the quiet mountain, the enlightened person finds his level through learning, decisiveness, and correct persistence.

And old chestnuts.

Another bump. Clouds of anxiety rise. Do not be anxious, but fly with confidence. Correct persistence brings progress.

We read to reveal ourselves. I discover as an Anglo-Celtic Australian, the term for me is a Skip, but skipping such a strange activity involving a rope originating from children imitating ropemakers jumping over ropes to retrieve lengths of hemp as they twist the strands to make the rope and being a Skip, I become strange and fascinating. Winky doubts this. Fact.

We land in Pudong, the strength of heaven supports winds of gradual change, smoothing the landing and the usual airport shit fight.

Listen. Restraint brings progress and satisfaction. Make minor changes to? The soul concealing all actions to avoid confrontation.

Easy. The Maglev train into Shanghai. The train's nickname, Madame White Snake.

The female announcer at the station, her anthropomorphic voice speaking in standard Mandarin, declaring the arrival of the Maglev. This condescending announcement. Imagine her words.

This is our clean fast train with nice comfortable cabins and cushioned seats. We are very satisfied with our beautiful shiny fast train, so smooth and silent much better than screeching hulking Western trains. Our trains are very superior to your trains. Our trains are faster than your trains. Your trains are too slow.

I love the slow.

This horizontal gleaming rocket zooms into the station. My aghast face reflects repeatedly in the fleeting windows. I turn to Benevolence.

If you tell me it's awesome, I'll kick you in the shins.

Of course, I wouldn't.

The receptive earth below our feet and profundity above, indicates the need for unity and a collective awareness of the goal, do not procrastinate, join with others, return to the plan. What is the plan.

Illusion has no conclusion.

This train of moods, Snake the bullet train, the word bullet making me a nervous extreme knowing the fact of no such thing as a slow bullet. Maglev, an unfinished name for a train and what the hell does Maglev mean. An abbreviation for magnetic levitation. Which sounds painful. The train levitates, not that high, on a magnetic field to counteract the effects of gravity. Is that safe? Must be. Hopeful. This train operates at a speed of four hundred and thirty kilometers an hour. Shit. Minor amounts of scary at first. Now the alarm kicks in. Not enchanted with the prospect of levitating on a magnetic field at the speed of light instead of chugging along in a nice normal train on a steady set of metal wheels firmly attached to the tracks and noisy some screeching the sound of brakes all good the stopping. A human person, well, it's not designed to move at such a speed except for oh manic flights of fancy. I avoid unnatural speed. The floating, the mysticism of levitation and we ride the levitating train with half a name and what is a magnetic whatever, it's the apocalypse, it's the end of times, it's the future and the past of dead babies and burning cash and this tug-o-war I prefer not to know.

The excessive below. The strong beyond. Separate the inferior and superior to achieve progress. Change gives way to stability.

Fine fine fine, my delightful playmate, a jolly romancer, the splendid Bogart soul, Benevolence says,

Stick with me kid.

What about the lubricity of my brain, muscles, internal organs, the fluids, my nervous cells? Every molecule of my body brakes in unison. This effort to slow down throws my organs into complete disarray. In the wake of light speeding, impossible to escape how fast we go, for at the head of the carriage, a lighted screen of red flashing numbers relays the ever-increasing kilometers, like the countdown to an explosion. Ignore. Close my eyes. But it's flashing inside my head. Stop. This feud of fast and slow.

Gaze at a dull grey landscape, a place to forget, incapable of distracting from flashes. Numbers burn like a branding iron argh. Try to convince myself this Maglev remains stationary, not going anywhere. Look, it's the outer suburbs, the factories, freeways, rivers, canals, boxy houses and metallic poles racing past us. A pink industrial building flies by! The passionate color, a shock in this monochrome expanse. Then a claret tin roof, the color of my nose, a square of green grass following a red as red as veins, advertisement plastered with the geometric flowers of Chinese characters. In the distance, moving closer and closer, approximately thirty blocks of rigid apartments standing together, symbol of strength in numbers, as if just risen from the tarmac, the car parks and the rows of half-dead leafless trees. A concrete bridge appears out of nowhere dragging a red truck. The bridge curves in an arc and rushes over the top of the train. Up pops an oversized billboard, an image of a happy family, beaming, grandparents, Mom and Dad and one blank-faced boy-child, all three wearing matching sweaters, hands on shoulders, grouped beside an English word cloud, ME YOU HIM HER JOY. Five minutes of blank, have they erased, no another billboard springs to life, a garden of sunflowers surround a happy couple leaning close together with a boy nestling in their laps, all three pointing to Chinese characters splashed across a Byzantium sky, 'Dream Abortion, Totally Painless.'

The city wobbles, rocks and jolts, but not me! In the stillness of my still, I will not be moved as the ragged suburbs of Shanghai flick by in an instant, as I pretend the motionless Maglev goes nowhere. I am going nowhere, the reason for travel, be calm and exist within my own reality.

Opposite me, sits the excited, thrilled, red-faced, bright-eyed, grinning Benevolence, dying to shriek *awesome*.

The Puxi again, Pudong again, Puxi again poetry, the Pudong district on the east side of The Huangpu River dividing Shanghai. And in this body of water who discovers the carcasses of two thousand eight hundred pigs? The waste.

Domestic sewage, industrial discharges, ships'refuse pollutes this city caught between poetry and pig pollution. Pigs with massive brains, want peace of mind, they forage, they anticipate, they empathize, they do not deserve to die.

Today. The Air Quality Index, a throat searing, tear duct overflowing, 400. A level indicating hazardous. Don't hold your breath.

Shanghai, hey Paris of the East, above the sea. City of hen-pecked husbands, copy cats, cunning businessmen, lack of facial hair, lovers of sugar and money money money.

Smoke a jade stem pipe and dream. Where are the rice fields, the empress dowagers, the coolies, the lanterns, the impassive stares, the bamboo thickets, the peasants bearing baskets on a yoke. In the dim light of evening, a tuneless song of humanity. A caterwaul.

Chinese women cultivate pallid complexions believing fair skin conceals a thousand flaws, a beauty untouched by the indignity of the laboring peasant. So, cover your face with chiffon scarves, surgical masks or tinted shields. Long sleeves, wrist to arm length gloves and trousers, protect bare skin from the sun. Apply bleaching creams Discoloration Reversal Moisturizer, White Rush, Lightening Whitening, Pink Daisy Anal Bleaching. This promise of aristocratic paleness. The poet Du Mu writes, 'Even the people on the street look lifeless.'

Where can I buy a bottle of wine in Shanghai?

In Shanghai, merchants nap at midday, everyone sleeps anytime of the day or night, wherever they are. Security guards doze in tipped back chairs. Priests rest face down on park benches. Shoe cobblers put their feet up and snooze. Taxi drivers fall asleep at the wheel. A profound peace on their sleeping faces. Rising at four and the exhausted permanently stooped from the weight of produce and leather eyes looking down, sit on the pavement, on a step and tear the outer sheaths from stalks of corn, claw the monotony, fall asleep do not snore and wake to clack chopsticks in bowls of rice. Stay away while Shanghai sleeps. Sleep lingers above a whole life. Walk, tread soft, with tender feet everywhere except. Do not wake the billions.

Thames Town an imitation English town, complete with cobbled streets, red phone boxes, Tudor houses, an English pub, and a spooky gothic church. A deserted and decaying place, nobody wants to live in this ghost town. We won't go there.

On Sundays, the coal barges head upstream. High-rise buildings shoot from the ground overnight. It's laundry day every day. A constant flux of here today gone tomorrow, leaking buildings, bamboo scaffolding, shopaholic paradise. Hello. The Alexander Pushkin statue on the corner of Dongping Lu and Fenyang Lu Grandparents sweep the streets. Vampire coffee comes with a nitrous oxide injection. Eat chocolate coffin cakes, witches fingers cookies. Wear pajamas in public. The toilet cafe offers food the texture of poo (not going there either).

On weekends, sweet-tooth parents crowd People's Park in search of husbands and wives for their unmarried children.

Hail high-rise Shanghai! Chock full of glass and steel skyscrapers. Do I want to sleep seventy floors above solid ground? No. Burning bodies, not pretty.

Choose a boutique hotel in The French Concession, the heart of a colonial area, plane trees, mansard roofs and shuttered windows. This hotel once the headquarters of vice boss Du Yuesheng. Once the nerve center of an opium empire. Host to countless decadent parties. Glamorous gangsters beckon. And men grown from foreign trade, play drinking games all night, while courtesans stoke their opium pipes.

This hotel, not quite Salt Melon Street or Chessboard Street. Plush carpets and heavy satin drapes in the lobby, make mysteries possible. Faint smells of rice wine and cedar polish mingle with the sound of a gruff Fats Waller singing, Ain't Misbehavin. Screens carved in bamboo motifs curve around purple velvet sofas. Silk scrolls of mists obscuring plum blossoms, weeping willows and mountain peaks. An ivory bodhisattva and jade snuff bottles decorate a fireplace mantle. Antique gramophones, telephones, typewriters, yellowing sheets of music sweep us back to the golden era of the 1920's.

The petite silk slippers embroidered with Beijing knots. Slippers sewn for folded feet, a symbolic reminder of the cruelty inflicted on Chinese women hobbling on broken stumps. Women bind a girl's feet, her best chance to improve herself and find good fortune. Feet take the shape of perfect lilies. And delicate stitches outline swallows in flight.

Recline on a plump velvet chair in Room 214. Long journey sips Jasmine tea from a porcelain cup. Open a brochure and read this description of the Chinese tea ceremony.

Tea ceremony is just like the moon, the human mind is just like the thousands of waters and the tea thick as bitter medicine is just like our life, the experience of life need we tea drinkers to know with time flies. When drinking tea, people enjoys the hominoids beauty between human and nature, without noisy and dispute, a kind of elegance for molding a persons' temperament, including quiet and beautiful drinking, with the flies and the refined tastes of gathering.

I wonder what 'the hominoids beauty' means.

The hotel bathroom features the Intelligence Toilet, an electronic toilet like a giant electric bread maker. A toilet wiser than humans. A toilet so complicated it is inoperable, flummoxing

Simplicity standing in front of it with her legs crossed. Try
to decipher each function lit by a row of red lights. *Energy
saving. Seat temperature. Rear spray. Water lamp. Auto flush. Air
dry. Nozzle spray.* Push every button. Wait for the green lights
hoping green means 'on.' The lights turn the color of pee after
a night of heavy drinking. Two of the lights blink impatiently.
An urgent sound of water hissing. Warm air rushes from inside
the toilet bowl. Yikes. Take a step back. The toilet grows angry.
Horrid gurgling noises fill the bathroom. This revving toilet of
raging energy. The seat warms up. The lid closes automatically,
an expression of regal rage, as if to say. Enough.

On the rooftop bar of love, warm gentle breezes, distant
views of a temple with peacock-blue domes in the shape of
onions and behind a glinting Shanghai of dancing Chinese
characters against a dark sky remember clink clink champagne
glasses. Kanpei. Bottoms up.

Benevolence and Simplicity, two laowai, white-ghost
Westerners walk along Nanjing Road, number one street in
China. From all directions, hawkers rush towards us what the
hell. Eight blokes wave manila folders and shout,

Bags watches bags watches Bags watches bags watches
Bags watches bags watches Bags watches bags watches Bags
watches bags watches take a look you buy you buy you buy
you buy you buy you buy.

No thank you, over and over then shout, get away from
me. The harassment escalates. Besieged at every street corner,
Simplicity develops a strategy. I use Benevolence as a human
shield. The minute an enthusiastic group of hawkers appear,
dive behind Benevolence, grip his elbows and maneuver him
through the jostling mayhem.

The tour brochure promises, *One Day Wonderful Shanghai,
Morning Wonderful Shanghai. Afternoon Wonderful Shanghai.*

This brochure says, *The old French Concession area with old streets and old houses, an old stone gateway and original exteriors retaining the old appearance.* Old is good now in Shanghai. Old me, the original exterior, old body, old face. Keep telling myself, old is good as I trot about on flat unbound feet.

And shopping. Brittle shop assistants, the click of high heels, hands hide glossy lips. screaming, Aeeeeyoowwww, Shanghainese for, Holy Mother of God look at that fat bignosed spotty white-ghost woman.

Vehicles clog roads with a complete disregard for traffic regulations. Motor bikes, taxis, trucks, silent scooters and millions of bicycles obey their own set of road rules. This dreamlike slowness, swerving around obstacles, people, anything in the way. Riders without helmets, spines ramrod straight, three or four to a scooter, weave in and out of lanes, drift from left to right, on the wrong side of the road, up onto footpaths, taking me by surprise, ignoring red lights, one-way streets, crosswalks, lane divisions and pedestrians. Five cars travel abreast on a three-lane highway. Tricycles loaded with rubbish collected from street corners and demolished buildings and a mass of crushed cardboard boxes, old mattresses, metal poles, frames, bags bulging with mysterious objects, these treasures tied with red rope.

Wet spells, intermittent showers, air dense with moisture, breathe water not oxygen, in the plum rains, even the mold rains, storm drains well up in thunderstorms, locals pirate electricity from street poles and escalators and it's cricket fighting season, pluck five inch insects from fields, in the summer months, cricket breeders grow one hundred thousand crickets trained for warfare and the Golden Autumn Cricket Lovers club meets every two weeks.

Climb the steep steps of the potbelly Shanghai Museum, the shape of a ding, a bronze cooking vessel. A line of Chinese men, women and children maybe five hundred people snaking out from the double doors and continuing down a path and along the street. At the exit to the museum shop, automatic doors open and Simplicity pushes Benevolence into the store. Buy a couple of souvenirs. Leave through the shop entrance into the lobby and sidestep to the head of the queue without looking at hundreds of fuming Chinese faces and walk straight into the main hall of the museum and not feel guilty.

Keep the business card for Jenny's Bloo Bai on Donghue Road okay get tipsy nice term for drunk, shall we go back to Jenny's Bloo Bai on Donghue Road. Give the card to a helpful person. On the back of the card is a map and the words, Please take me to JENNYS.

Two tulle wedding dresses hang from the electric lines over the sidewalk. In this humidity, white satin imagines jilted at the temple alter, wash those unsaid vows, keep the dress for the next time, lonely net softens the blow and gentle rustlings hanging out to dry.

The stone mosaics, carved stone flowers, a leering dragon, the snake-like body rippling across a terra cotta rooftop, flames rise from the arches of its reptilian back, head rearing, the mouth open, I hear screaming.

Excerpts from a Shanghai Municipal Tourism Administrative Commission leaflet on Shanghai Parks and Gardens.

Shanghai Wild Animal Park. *In the bus visiting area you can see the beasts of prey walking around freely. In the walking area you can get in close touch with meek fowls and birds.* Shanghai Century Park. *Mainly consists of large plots of lawns, forests and lakes and is divided into seven areas: a pastoral garden, a viewing terrace, a beach area, a tree-spaced lawn, birds preserving area, an international flowers area, and a mini-golf course and enjoys the reputation of Park for Holiday.*

Changfeng Park. *Among the twenty special scenes of this park are green maples in the oasis, sunset, three friends in cold winter (pine, bamboo and plum).* Autumn Glow Garden. *It is said, Emperor Quianlong spoke highly of a cooking named silver claw soft-shelled turtle.* Guilin Park. *During the mid-autumn, the park is featured by the fragrance of the blossoms.* Dongping National Forest Park. *The main service items and facilities are a field tent, a forest hammock, a beach swimming pool, grass skating, rock climbing, horse riding, kart.*

A walk in the park, visiting a family of paper pandas in a thicket of bamboo, rows of paper and wire lanterns strung across the path, lanterns in the shape of vegetables and heads of animals, a giant chili pepper beside a brown legless rabbit, a grinning mouse head with a pink nose and lime green ears, a brown monkey head with three eyelashes stuck to each eyelid, a diamond shaped strawberry, a bee, a pumpkin and a devil with teardrop horns.

A walk in the. Another lush. Lobelia bordering a lake, a cluster of fake cows with udders dangling three teats like deflated penises and gloss black and white skin, a Dalmatian pattern, as if perpetually wet, shines today in the light drizzle, sculpted eyes looking in different directions, serene and lady-like, enjoying their surroundings, deep in discussion. Do the cows remain in the same positions forever or does the park keeper move them about in the middle of the night.

A walk full of flowers, magnolias, mottled bark, Chinese junipers and Hankow willows, two oversized metal stilettoes, amber and bone, Marigolds fill both shoes in front of three metallic cut-outs of cheerful jesters and painted gnomes wearing Medieval outfits. In Shanghai, parks must be fun.

The Oriental Pearl Tower Radio and TV Tower in the Pudong district featured in the films Godzilla and Mission

Impossible, views of the whole of Shanghai, a revolving restaurant, transparent observatory, you'll love it.

But.

The man does not understand my fear of heights.

At the foot of The Oriental Pearl Tower, a row of flags flap primary colors. Giant pink pearls on legs of concrete tubes with silver joints. The highest pearl stuck on a neck in the shape of a tubular ladder. Think space-age satellite, Dr Spock at the helm. Benevolence happy at the prospect of another ascent into the heavens.

I might stay down here with the flags.

Nonsense.

Benevolence purchases two tickets. I read the list of rules pinned to the wall near the ticket office.

Notes For Entering The Tower.

1. The ragamuffin, drunken people and psychotics are forbidden to enter the tower.
2. No smoking at non-appointed spot.
3. Prohibit carrying tinder and exploder (banger, match, lighter) restricted cutter (kitchen knife, scissors, fruit knife, sword and so on) and metal made electronic appliance.
4. Prohibit carrying animals and the articles which disturb common sanitation (including the peculiar smell of effluvium.)
5. Prohibit carrying the articles which can destroy and pollute the inner environment of the tower.
6. Prohibit carrying dangerous germs, pests and other baleful biology. Forbid any articles from epidemic areas.
7. Prohibit hanging streamer slogan and any other prints in the tower, including commerce, politics, religion and so on.

8.   The cubage of liquid articles which the tourist carries can't exceed 100 milliliter. And the liquid article must be put at the appointed spot to accept examination. After confirmed it can be carried into the Tower. The interloper carrying contraband will be punished seriously by police.

Enter the humungous circular hall. Surprise. The first queue begins at the turnstile, streams across the hall onto the balcony and runs around the circumference of the interior. This spectacle of organized humanity. And it's too late for us to turn back. Two hours of shuffling. Simplicity busting to pee. Enter a cramped tunnel packed with wall-to-wall human sardines, elbows in ears, faint smells of body odor and garlic breath. Squeeze our way along the tunnel leading to six piddling elevators servicing hundreds of people. Three hours later, wobble on shaking legs onto the viewing deck onto the glass floor help me I am standing on air above this immense city, luminous behind a veil of smog. Far below on the flat putty Huangpu River with several barges pasted to its surface. A few ferries wend their way from one side to the other. An ocean liner docks at the cool dock, that is all. This sluggish river no longer jammed with liners, cargo ships, sampans and junks with ribbed sails like bats' wings. From the Tower, the barges filled with sand, appear delicate, all facing the same direction like cells seen through a microscope.

Dusk. The dusky Bund of western style building facades of granite and stone of marble columns reflecting the golden rays of sunset lalala. The old neighborhoods disappear. Dismantle makeshift shanty towns and replace with steel and concrete monsters. View of the tower on the far side of the river. Position Benevolence directly in front of the now distant Oriental Pearl Tower. The tower sprouts from the top of his head. Take a photograph. Tourist ha.

The fabric market. Industrious Chinese men and women bend over sewing machines and yank the fabric under stabbing needles and cough and spit and feet treadle scattering scraps of cloth onto the floor. Bales of cloth crowd each stall's stifling atmosphere in the heat. Rancid smells mix with the heavy scent of incense smoldering on alters. Impassive faces, imploring eyes. Stall holders hold out garments.

We makee for you missy special for you come big big size see missus madam come see here come see perfection for you.

Yes. Thank you. Perfect for me.

I cannot breathe.

A Shanghai café serves coffee in a Royal Belgian Balancing Siphon Coffee Maker. A structure of gold brass mechanisms and ballooning glass containers set on a wood base, dating back to the 1830's. This coffee maker uses gravity and vacuum principles. Turn off the faucet on the brass cylinder. Fill the boiler chamber (glass balloon) with hot water. Add ground coffee powder in the heavy glass brew chamber. A tube connects the two chambers. The weight of water causes the boiler to sit low on the swing frame. Press the weighted counterpoise. Open the lid of the spirit lamp alcohol wick burner. Light it. The water boils forcing itself into the brewing chamber. The boiler rises. All hail the rising boiler. The lid of the burner closes extinguishing the flame and creates a vacuum inside the boiler, drawing the brewed coffee from the brewing chamber back into the boiler. Turn on the faucet on the brass cylinder. Serve coffee from the tap. The fine mesh filter covers the tube connecting the chamber never needs replacing. Enjoy the entire process, a visual spectacle. Enjoy the coffee. Which tastes the same as other coffee.

The dowdy department store full of flesh colored underpants and singlets and dust and as I leave, a van pulls up outside. Six men like a gang of sextuplets toting machine guns and dressed in black military fatigues, leap out of the van and run up the steps into the store. From bland to admiration, such neat uniforms, such trim armed men. And the overkill. Sending these robo-cops to arrest a shoplifter or worse. I skulk away not wanting to be caught in the line of fire.

This city of a million noises. Can you hear the beating of a brass gong, the sound of a melancholic bugle, the strident falsetto from a distant slum or a beggar's whine beyond help rags in tatters and the crowds of endless shoving?

Stuff ourselves into a crowded train and I read the sign on the automatic train door.

Caution: Risk of Pinching Hands.

I look around at the commuters, thieves, perverts pressing against each other. What will they pinch? Bottoms? Upper arms? Bags? The steam coming from my ears?

I know now and the realization takes years. The sign means the danger of hands being caught in the door.

Sip my tea just like the moon. Like thousands of waters. With the experience of life, need we tea drinkers to know with time flies our quiet and beautiful drinking with the flies and the refined tastes gathering around zithers, many players plucking the strings to create the sounds of objects that do not make sounds. Bamboo, silk, clay.

China, a mystery to us and us a mystery to China and Shanghai a conglomeration of the word cloud ME YOU HIM HER JOY, of screeching shop assistants, temperamental toilets, leering dragons, lanterns with unblinking eyes, brass gongs clanging in forgotten temples, the yin and the yang of upturned eves, shiny cows, ragamuffins, baleful biology, interlopers carrying contraband and the risk of pinching hands, encapsulates a China of how Westerners imagine China to be. Exquisite, shrouded in mist, foul odors, amusing, noisy, illogical, pushing, eating at all hours, barbers scraping under eyelids and the cowlicks in the men's cropped hair creates a tiny white space on the back of their heads.

Philosophers and Leeches

Ancient water town Suzhou. The National Day Golden Week. What could be better? A hot rainy seven day holiday of one point three billion people visiting cities and tourist destinations and unknown to me, a date to avoid traveling in China.

We'll take the train.

What about. Violence and altercations as a result of overcrowding.

The day, not golden, but grey sleet. Side step puddles. Join a crowd of twenty million Chinese citizens shuffling into Shanghai Hongqaio Railway Station, yes a frenetic atmosphere. Everyone rushes past me dawdling and allowing people to go ahead of me at the turnstile. Benevolence shoves me through. Ow.

You have to push.

We enter a kind of holding pen furnished with rows of hard metal seats. Men and women smoke, stare at mobile phones, read the paper, feed the children. Are there children? I remember. Silence. Everybody eating noiselessly. Nobody speaking. No conversations. Oh god. The calm before the, will there be mass hysteria, queues form near yet more turnstiles, this limiting and controlling of the exit, which is the point of a turnstile, also to baffle, to create a gateway in one direction, one person at a time, a seething race begins as the train pulls into the station. Run. As if set free from a cage, everyone elbowing us down the stairs to our, thank god, reserved seats.

The rain-spattered train window. Paddy fields, muddy ditches, overgrown bamboo groves and the occasional shrine, the roof curling upwards. A group of kids wave sticks at the passing train. Not the children of beggars. These children shout and grin, making insolent faces. Do they learn in school history how starving peasants stole dead babies to beg with? Brandishing tiny corpses at bystanders, locals and travelers and wailing,

Baby hungry.

Marco Polo visited Suzhou in 1276. He wrote,

Suju [i.e., Suzhou] is a very great and noble city. The people are Idolaters, subjects of the Great Kaan, and have paper-money. They possess silk in great quantities, The city is passing great, and has a circuit of some 60 miles; it hath merchants of great wealth and an incalculable number of people. There are also in this city many philosophers and leeches, diligent students of nature. And you must know that in this city there are 6,000 bridges, all of stone, and so lofty that a galley, or even two galleys at once, could pass underneath one of them.

The tourist map sings water town Suzhou's praises, the Venice of the East, the many arched bridges span polluted rivers crisscrossing the city.

Zhou Zhuang is the NO 1 water village in China. Small bridges, Running Waters, Old Houses. You will escape the huzzles and buzzles touching the genuine glamour with highlight of Water Town Show. And another activity is called Picking Pearl. Is it interesting to pick the shell from fresh water and open it to find pearls of you?

Our tour guide, Liang, appears vacuous, her flour-dipped dim sum features, drowsy eyes and dumpy legs.

We board a gondola and glide through the stagnant canals of, not so noble, Suzhou. Grimy blackened cottages built in the Ming and Qing dynasties cling to the edge of narrow waterways. Dense dwellings align like the teeth of a comb or spreading out like a chessboard. Rotting refuse fills open drains. Bulging bags of rubbish, rusting bicycle wheels, upturned tin dishes, milk crates, broken baskets on random rooftops. Limp clothes hang from bamboo washing lines, no pegs.

And the bamboo walkways, red lanterns, red flags, red lacquered junks, more red flags, a man in a singlet scales a fish, a cane chair nailed to a wall, flying bridges like rainbows, arched bridges like Venice but nothing like Venice, thousands of tiled roofs think fish scales. The sandy tin roofs of barges low in the water. Children wave at us from barges. Chang gate straddles the spoiled streams. The Precious Belt Bridge stretches across a canal. Carved periwinkle birds adorn boats floating backwards and forwards. What ruin terraces, willow trees new, a clear chant of songs and a spring unbearable.

Thin mists float with breeze in mulberry Suzhou. Children follow grandpas to grow melons in mulberry shade. Cold shivers rise from the ravine. These courteous and moral people don't ask me how, life in their faces from history and humidity. Teach children diction and calligraphy. The old people cannot distinguish a dagger from a lance. But no serious banditry in this city seen as the Paradise of China.

So to the grime slime markets selling water chestnuts, lotus roots and dried chili. Fill buckets with crawling black crabs trapped under green netting. A row of live ducks, their feet tied to the tops of wire cages. Cruel image defying gravity.

A tanned man, not a wrinkle in sight, wears a white singlet and sleeps like a newborn on twenty kilo bags of dried dog food. One arm flung over his head. A tin teapot by his side. Try not to look at intestines, slimy organs filling steel dishes. Containers of dark eggs with a web of veins covering the shells, marinating in turgid liquid. Gah. Queasy buckets of bloodied fish heads, platters of chicken fat, a blood spattered chopping board, jars of cloven hoofs. Normal delicacies for the people. But no thank you. Thanks for offering.

A crowd gathers in front of a doorway. One woman wears a pair of cotton pajamas. Other bra-less women with helmet grey hair, wear plain buttoned up shirts calmly posing for. A man slings a camera on his shoulder for. Wait here for.

The bride and groom.

The barber shop, one spare chair, the door ajar reveals sadness at the futility against humidity hits rough, the lack of hygiene defeats, but life anyway must get a haircut. This plain barber trims an old man's thin hair. Snip. Should snap this scene, raise my Nikon. The barber slams the door shut. Go away. Leave us in peace. To go about our lives. You are different. Aliens, yes, fish out of water in Suzhou.

Liang takes us to a silk mill. Piles of bamboo trays hold hundreds of fat baby silkworms munching happily on mulberry leaves. Life-size dolls sit at wooden looms, this display of what it once was. Quiet. Looming. The mannequins wear cherry and lime colored silk. Mannequins smile how charming. How cheerful. How self-fulfilling. But the real weavers wear plain white shirts and black pants and stand spinning the thread from dead pupa on mechanical machines making a deafening noise. Do heads spin? Still everyone is happy.

Dystopian Tiger Hill lies to the west of ancient Suzhou. The brochure says,

Tiger Hill has the reputation of being the No 1 sight of Suzhou. Tiger Hill, a lure and beauty of its own, combines perfectly the picturesque scenery with cultural legacies. It is brilliant, uncommon cultural treasure of humanity. Tiger Hill is an important meeting place for The Summer Enjoyment of Coolness Fair and The Autumn Sweet Osmanthus Fair. There are three most wonderful viewing places and nine different ways of enjoying it under nine different weather conditions and eighteen sights of the hill. It can match its beauty against other famous mountains and rivers. Under the sword Pool concealing the secrets of the Tomb of King Wu with his valuable swords, with the windy dale and cloudy springs, making visitors reluctant to leave.

The summer enjoyment.
The Song poet Su Dongpu wrote,
It would be a pity if you had been to Suzhou but didn't get to visit the Tiger Hill and see The Broken Beam Temple, The Sword Testing Stone and The 1000 Men's Rock Villa with a thousand Scenes.

Lu Yu Well wrote, The Treatise of Tea, while living on Tiger Hill and picking tea blossoms in the evening crimson clouds of spring.
Where the Yunyan Ta leaning pagoda, one hundred and fifty eight feet high and leans three hundred and fifty nine

degrees northwest of Benevolence ascending and waving to me from the top.

Wanjing Villa. Holidaymakers crowd the bonsai park. Arrange proud bonsai trees on cement pillars, space evenly over the grounds. The two elements of the refined and precise art of bonsai, the concept of tree and pot. Suppress growth, manipulate and stunt the roots. Dwarf trunks and branches gnarling like arms sprout a cluster of leaves. Creates these characteristics of aloofness, generosity, sparseness, austerity and unpretentious inner strength what to aspire to for the result of tortured trees proves containment as the defining feature. Captures this essence of nature. *Certainly Sun and Moon are in the sky framed by this little pot.* And the foliage of masculine bonsai resembles umbrella shapes. A shock of pine needle erupts from the limbs of feminine bonsai. Ah my tears water the helpless trees.

Aesthetic birdhouses slip into rock niches.

A sign inserted into a bunch of rocks,
Slippery in Rainy Day, Caution!
And another sign in a garden bed requests,
Please Don't Climb Trees and Pick Flowers for The Sake of Life.

Not far from Tiger Hill, we find The Surging Waves Pavilion what it is in the morning mists and pebble streams and ringing a marble bell for chime celebrates mountain and forest and not remembering Garden of the Master Of Nets.

The Humble Administrator's Garden. Clumps of cream dahlias, waterfalls, white water lilies surround a miniature village facing the broad expanse of a lake, poetic landscapes, waterscapes, with exquisite buildings, luxuriant vegetation varies at every step. Awaken reminiscences of Venetian scenes really this Humble Administrator of the archaic, rustic, extensive and naturalistic. A map of the garden illustrates emerald grass, aqua lakes, pagodas, temples and a red dot states,

Your present position and listed below.
A secluded and fragrant and lingering and delightful in snow pointing angelic position.
The Secluded Temple of Firmiana Simplex and Bamboo
The Hall Of Distant Fragrance the faint scent of osmanthus.
The House of Sweet-Smelling Rice
Lingering Garden
The Delightful Pavilion of True Delight
The Standing-in-Snow Hall
The Pointing at Cypress Hall
The Angelic Prunus Mume and Lotus Blooms House
A sign, three lines of Chinese characters and below the characters, clear black instructions in English.
Potential danger is worse than naked fire.
Precaution before salvation.
Fire can be devastating.

Go enjoy reading 'The No-Word Tablet.' Quote.
Originally there had been words related to Taoism in the tablet with strong strokes written by Fang Xiaoru. Later Zhu-ld usurped the powers becoming empower, he ordered Fang to write the imperial edict, but Fang refused therefore Fang and his relatives were killed. All the words in his tablet were cleaned up, so it became a no-word tablet. Now the originally engraved words are hardly visible, but this tablet embodies the upright spirit of Mr Fang.

upright
spirit
embodies

Lily pads the size of car tires in a pond, a pine boat floats past, in a pond, an audience of a thousand lily parasols balance on stalks surrounding, in a pond, this sea of crowded gentleness.

I photograph letters painted on a rough wooden beam, Take Care Of Your Head. But a head takes care of itself. And what's inside, a stew of wits and puns.

In China, a name explains what everything and halls.

The Small Flying Rainbow Bridge
The Floating Green Tower
Hall of Pure Trinity
Hall of God of Wealth
Hall of God of Literature
Hall of Avalokiteshvara
Hall of God of Longevity
Hall of Four-Auspicious Merits

A diminutive Chinese man trots past us and disappears behind The Mountain-in-View Tower. His incredulous face abruptly reappears from behind the tower. He gawps at the sight of the chunky Westerners. The round green eyes, wide mouth, full lips and big belly of Benevolence mountain man and Simplicity, his plump concubine. The man whips out his camera. Quick, take a picture. Of the two beefy and buxom foreign devils we are. A shock to the pipsqueak peasants from the provinces.

China makes me self-conscious. I'm forced to keep my arms across my chest like I'm in a strait jacket. It's these watermelon boobs. The men stare at my breasts.

Winky's eyes twinkle.

Really? I haven't noticed.

The morning of our second day in Suzhou. Liang asks,

What do you want to buy here I take you?

Curtains.

Liang claps her hands.

No one ever asked this before.

A tin warehouse, the size of a football stadium. A boundless space of clammy shops selling curtains. Ugly net, nylon, synthetic curtains. Force a smile. Grim. What to do without creating an international incident? I stop in front of a shop window and point.

Those.

Damask drapes. Cream and charcoal colors weaving a fleur de lis pattern and fit for a French chateau. And those heavy Regency pair, satin embroidered with olive and gold lotus flowers, and tassels trimming a cambric lining. Benevolence and Liang negotiate a price. One hundred dollars. An ecstatic shopkeeper wraps all four curtains and at no extra cost, throws in the tiebacks, enormous Botticelli baubles fringed with silky threads attached to cords. How shall we cope with the weight?

The last night in Suzhou on the hotel balcony still for a short time following the blazing moon disappearing behind a pagoda lit with scarlet lights.

Ram thirty kilos of curtains into my suitcase.

October 1st 2009 the sixtieth anniversary of the founding of the People's Republic of China. Ten thousand military troops march somewhere. Displays of high-tech weapons. Parades of one hundred thousand people. A pageant of brilliant achievement here beautiful prosperous China sings, Our Great Motherland is a Garden, I Love China, Emancipated Serfs Sing Proudly, Folk Songs Are Like Spring Water, The Sunny Way, Firmly We Hold Our Hands.

The newsreader describes Hu Jintao's bulletproof limousine as incorporated with distinctive Chinese elements. The taillights of the limo resemble ancient palace lanterns and the radiator grill in the shape of a Chinese folding fan. But the car seems to grow, baring teeth, the sunny way.

Shanghai station. Benevolence cannot fit the suitcase packed with curtains through the train station's narrow turnstile. The case being too heavy to lift over the top of the turnstile, Benevolence pushes it underneath and sweating and swearing, he crawls on his hands and knees on the filthy ground under the barrier much to the fascination of twenty million astonished Chinese commuters.

Finish on a good note

These notes and stories. They. Wing me over the sea and the universe unites in power and a wise woman executes her actions with creativity and exceptional progress comes by correct persistence and. Remember diversity.

A time comes for me to. Begin.
Everything is booked.
Live safe.
And live on in flowers.
To bloom within our own odyssey.
If I owned a car like that, I would get in and drive it somewhere I am not, someplace else.
Stick with me kid.
Reason enough to be born on this planet.

About the Author

Judyth Emanuel's debut novel YEH HELL OW was published February 2019. Her writing has been described as innovative and important work. She is one of three winners in 2017 Victoria University Short Story Prize for New and Emerging Writers. She has short stories in anthologies and literary journals including Electric Literature Recommended Reading, Overland, Hobartpulp, Literary Orphans, Jellyfish Review, Into The Void, Entropy, No Alibis Press 2019 Anthology, Longleaf Review, Adelaide Literary Magazine, Bending Genres and elsewhere.

Judyth Emanuel graduated BA Visual Communications, BA Fine Arts and MFA in Creative Writing.

She has lived in Kuwait, Saudi Arabia, London, Cyprus and Boston and now lives in Sydney, Australia and New York City.

www.ingramcontent.com/pod-product-compliance
Lightning Source LLC
Chambersburg PA
CBHW021436020726
47499CB00006BA/2027